An
Unabridged
Book of
Good and
Evil

XVE

Books by xve:

Letters to Dandelion

The Arizona Papers

Black Sheep's Soul

An Unabridged book of
Good and Evil

The Pathos Wars

An Unabridged Book of Good and Evil

XVE

xve

Publications

Proof of God's existence is simple...

No one dead or alive

young or old

rich or poor

obtains

Heaven on Earth.

An Unabridged Book of Good and Evil

An Unabridged Book of Good and Evil

Alt Cover Concept

THE BAD

HERE WE GO NOW...

Broken Glass

Can you see these words, flying at you like broken glass?
Stilettos, jagged and scattered as through a shotgun blast.

Hit the deck bitch, Grim Reaper's really coming –

Price on your head, want you dead, your blood'll soon be running.

Cold.

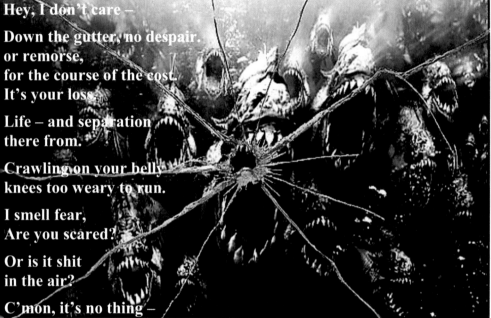

Hey, I don't care –

Down the gutter, no despair.
or remorse,
for the course of the cost.
It's your loss.

Life – and separation
there from.

Crawling on your belly
knees too weary to run.

I smell fear,
Are you scared?

Or is it shit
in the air?

C'mon, it's no thing –
People die everyday
well - maybe just not this way.

but hey

I'm only a paid gun – This is actually sort of fun
-- till yea it's my turn.

SHA-CLACK – Remington's ready.
Feel the heat. Satan's prepared a final meal for the depraved.
The Angel's chorus warms up for your great departures' paved.

"Oh God, Oh Please!" You scream before you leave,
- in a final breath heaved

BAM!

Silence chills the night.

Your head now left from right and what a fucked up, ugly sight

headless corpse choking hard for life,
though an overexposed windpipe and
muscles sans bones and sinews to cling to.

Fingernails scrape, digging into the concrete,
a last ditch effort pointless-completes

St. Peter you'll soon meet,
and your desperate movements
so deplete
– the fun.

I dowse my ciggy butt in your creeping blood –
wipe away my sweat, like a flood
and then a strange moment unfolds

Just who the fuck were you anyway?

Could I be so wrong
to contemplate loving doing this all day long

I should have listened better in math class.

Cause now it's my ass,

as my car runs on gas …

and not blood.

Crystal Castles

are those things that we think we can't live without
or those titles many believe gives major clout
the carefree times living life in - zero doubt
are what I define as building - crystal castles.

"Anthem Times," a verse written long time ago
in a mindset so now far, far away – a different
tone to which could result a tome of information
as to how I thought in those days of paltry youth.   *(Castle long demolished...)*

I've seen them in all their splendor and captivating
glory – i.e. – *The Crystal Cathedral* – a monolith
and juggernaut of the so-called religious era – soon
to be a fine Japanese eatery or a Buddhist Temple.

What a literal example – of a Crystal Castle and its
structured-tenured tear-filled collapsing downfall.

God has no fucking sense of humor on this one –
I rarely quote the Bible *direct* but it is quite clear –
*"Have no one before me, father, mother, daughter
son, lover, dog or centipede,"* – *"Let the dead bury
the dead,"* according to Jesus so trust me –
he might take great pleasure and gets immense glory
 – in ransacking the very shit outta that which you
wrap your arms clung around so tightly.

A Mexican proverb states – *You cannot accept
something new with your arms tourniquet-tied
around the world* – payoff – a Hand must be free
to receive something new.

So, many people – build the *"comfortable life"* –
then *(laugh)* – "*say*" they rebel against comforts.

Some people – advise on things they've never seen
nor knew about – but ask them the faintest real
facts and they have just no f'n clue.

Some folks love, love love the trophy wife,
the high life, the regal husband, the shithead

kids, the drama of politics, the daily grind,
the status of being a somebody – finally –

The ability to be *2-kool-for-skool* by talking
shit about all the budget trips that they took –
pushing the next poor slob out of the way
to get that picture with a very bleary-teary
eyed and pissed off Lion Cub.

Bunch of fucking White-bread-American assholes
I'd love to kick in your fucking door, roust your
disheveled ass out of bed and then snap a picture
with you like a fuckwad tourist.

All these things that seem so important and precious
are envious – pious – and eventually come crashing down.

And what a sight to see – I've quite seen a few – and been
inside plenty of my own – as when the lease is revoked and
the wrecking ball struck as both God and the Devil are there
high-fiving, arm-in-arm grinning like Cheshire Cats watching
as your shit gets Bulldozed by Fuck-U-R-Us to the ground.

I have to admit – the earth shaking and the glass
breaking, the window sills crumbling to sixty degree
angles, the floor caving in and the support beams shitting
downward as gravity takes hold.   All of this is just my
stupid analogies and garbage metaphors - so let me
give you actual some examples of some which I really seen…

Your wonderful, smart, svelte husband comes home
and says – Honey I have cancer. (5-year fight leads to 10-years off your life.)
You come home and your wonderful, smart, svelte
husband has been home banging the babysitter.
Your wonderful, smart, svelte husband has lost all of
his millions and now you're a live-in punching bag – *ha* –
(*but, the drugs made him do it…*)

Your hot, beautiful wife – cheats on you. (typical as the Northwinds)
Your hot, beautiful wife – cheats on you with your Boss (hmmm…)
Your hot, beautiful wife – cheats on you with her drug dealer ex –
(*prompting you to kill yourself…*)

Your hot, beautiful wife – cheats on you with your Father
(*prompting you to lose it all...*)
Your hot, beautiful wife – cheats on you with Me...
(*really can't see any problems with that one...*)

And the list goes on and on –
Your beliefs – gets crushed
Your car – gets stolen (or wrecked)
Your kid – is a rebellious snot
Your kid is a fuckin loser
Your kid – dies of cancer

Your trade – has lost its' luster.
They are turning off the lights to a job you had for decades.
What to do now – you are old, stupid, slow, over-sexed and comfortable.

Chappelle said it best – Had Monica Lewinski inquired
Bill Clinton would have replied – *"Suck my dick, there's
a future in it….."* Prompting me to wonder where I'd
be if I banged my college English Professor... (*I digress...*)

It's those Crystal Castles that must be razed to the
ground and some of them – stand in people's lives
for years, decades even a century.

In my case – nothing ever could seem to take root.
A glass shard or two would start to grow and then
floouwie – it was swept away, leaving me standing
there with the wind in my hair and tears dried like
thorn-stickers to the corners of my eyes, under the
non-Tuscan, Melanoma-baking sun.

My fun has been on loan – like really – all of us.

I've borrowed against time
against emotions
against the right and the wrongs and levied hard
the tariffs and the purchases of – oh well – fuck it –
my lusts.

I'm a sinful man --, what can I really say...

but those Castles – yes the ones we built
are as deep-rooted a sin, as well..., sin itself.

I'm standing on a patch of scorched Earth hoping
that I can at least cry my way to a garden
or a mud hut
or a cardboard box and ...

– But when I look up –

at you and yours

– all I can do – is start to wonder...

and say in my mind

It'll be some noise

When it all comes

crashing down.

THE DEMON ON MY BED

Early I arose, the morning sun, quite dead.
Drank coffee black, to ease my aching head.
Booted my computer, a new day I'd dread.

Looked to my bedroom, sight; my eyes fed,
A tiny troll, face of crimson red,
sitting in darkness aloft my bed.

There he was, as still as a shadow.
A disfigurement to etch my tomorrows.

"You see me ?" he crustily asked,
In muffled voice, as if he wore a mask.

I blinked my eyes, my brain I tasked,
for an excuse, explanation or prayer,
as to how it was I could see this figure ?

Am I dead ? Is this hell ?
Maybe I just don't feel so well ?

"Child of flesh" he pressed,
*"You can see me, no guess,
or so horror stricken you would not be."*

*"I admire your home, your wife and the life
given to thee."*

*"My Father, brothers and I, watch you in wait,
Yes, a fallen saint, and would welcome you to our abode."*

"How pure say you are ? Question thyself hard."
*"Imagine. No good deed has man done. For in the end,
when all is gone, everything shall be shown."*

*"A demon, me, yes, what you see, we are here. Everywhere.
In the air and in the trees. And of course in your head
for your eyes do not fail you."*

*"Watch the things you say and do,
for time shall end. -- Soon."*

And with that, I watched him fade from sight, his visage
dissipated by the light, breaking through the window pane.
No demon is a soothsayer of truth, and by this writing,
I purge the incident from my brain.

Freestyle

You don't shoot blanks,
You don't shoot caps,
You don't shoot shit,
You don't shoot craps,

You don't even shoot your mouth off nigga
I just done seen to that.

What you do shoot
is fuk'n nwack

In a gun fight, nigga like you,
all he got to make i'a noise like
a chicken bone to snap

Nigga, My knuckles I crack,
and you think a hole in your
mother fucking chest I'a clap.

You wife-da bitch I slap and
you Mom I give her da fuck'n
clap. (Wif extra crab meat nigga…)

When I skin a nigga
I do it wif my teeth
rip his spinal column out
shorten his ma fuk'n reach.

Who you play'n wif nigga
they named a gun barrel
a breach.

Uneducated ass, sit down
and learn while I teach class

cause if you don't,

I'ma come get you

kill and eat you

It's that

mother fuckin

simple.

Go back to Class

You can't write,
or
Can't act,
or
Can't sing,
keep it up bitch -
n' you'll fuckin swing,

You're just a wanna be

- punchy clown

stood up straight so I can knock you down.

Back to the ground
where you belong.

Or underground,
so you can sing this song,
of my foot up, so deep up
your narrow ass.

As the dog takes a piss,
upon the grass,
this place that marks your fuckin grave,
you piece of shit, low life nigger slave,

and if you can't - see,
the words I type

I'll come on by, and rape your wife.

Now that I schooled,
your broke dumb ass,

Better know this -

GO BACK TO CLASS !

Last stop to nowhere

Come be with me instead
He said, as she crossed away
from the door

not knowing that secretly
inside her--, His words
fell from her ears
straight to the floor.

As the train streamed forward
carrying them destined
toward a secluded if not
murky fate

A tip of His hat
an outstretch of His hand
she looked at Him first
then touched His face

I love you He said
it's all that I have left

It's all that matters
it's all that there is
inside of My heart.

We began this journey together
and I want us never to part.

She kissed Him silently, as
a tear traversed her cheek

her silence to Him was
unnerving and inside He
wanted to ask her to speak

The train slugged to a stop
and He had said all that He
could think of and done all
or more than a Man might

Yet – He felt that this was
not, if ever, never enough

The scream of the whistle
the screech of the slowing
squealing tires,
steel shredding upon steel, –

couldn't match His horror
nor overtake His sickened
stomach

as she threw herself

under the wheels

LO

(And Lo the devil came walking…)

And Lo, the Devil came walking and spoke to me one night.

"Come join me forever, leave God; give up all your rights."

"Come bow your head down at my feet, and worship me, and sin."

"Come live the life of freedom, where I will always let you win."

"The price is very small; your soul is all I ask for."

*"Not that I have much use for it. I need it to win a bet
you see. I bet GOD you would be dumb enough,
to curse him and then bow down to me."*

*"But even if you don't join, it's cool, I understand. I often
wish I'd kept my mouth shut; I'm to die for this, after the
destruction of all land."*

*"But others, I have signed to the roster; on their way to me
they speed. I tricked them with a powder, or sex, or advice
on thievery."*

*"They listened to my weak ideas; in their tiny little brains
it sounded so true. I lied to them and tripped then up,
now in this life, they are through."*

*"They sit and rot in prisons, squirm and cry with diseases;
Flash and strut with illegal things, of all natures. From evil
came these things they possess, that cause envy among you."*

*"Believers of the faith, how I loathe you. To touch you once,
I would die for. To smell the burning stench of human flesh;
next to me, a treasure I shall soon savor."*

*"I am here **on this earth, the king and ruler**; this world, at
THIS TIME IS MINE. I am here your hunter and your chaser,
and WILL SPEAK to each and every one of you, at certain,
selected times."*

*"Listen to me, if you choose. My advice will ALWAYS lead you
astray. I am the Father of ALL lies. The dealer of ALL pain.
I come quick to KILL all good, an opposer of GOD, I now stand."*

*"For in the last days I will be locked away, And BURN with ALL
the evil from this land. So join me, YOU, reader. If you dare!
Or heed the advice of the cursed WORD and turn and FLEE from here."
"The ONE who typed this paper. A faithful servant of me, once
was he. But he one day looked me in the eye, after I twisted
and mangled his life and made him cry; So said he,-"*

*"Thy powerless Demon you are marked to die. In the end of this
world, you will pay the price for your crimes. I will watch
you burn. I will not burn with you, but run to warn the rest
of the sheep. For those who listen to me, I will gladly lead,
For those who DO NOT heed these words, I surely will not weep.*

*"I will hear you scream, from the fiery, bottomless pit, you will
be chained by the Lord Jesus Christ, and die deep down within it."*

*"For you, a tear, I would never weep, NOT EVER, even to
quench your burning, lying tongue. I will look down from
above with the other ANGELS and watch you and your
CREW FRY until you are done."*

*"I speak such hatred of you, for the pain you've caused my life.
The chaos you brought to this world.
The death and destruction each and every day and night."*

To those who read this passage, the devil's time is near.
Do not accept the mark, even if threatened to be cut from
ear to ear. pray and hold on, wicked times are yet to follow.

Keep your eyes locked on God and keep reaching for tomorrow.

The devil is a powerless imp, no man, without God's permission,
is there that can be touched.

Save Job, who he laid his hand on, and caused him trouble
by much. The lying, cheating devil; a cursed little brat.
He can only whisper in your ear; it's bad he can even do that.

Because weaker minds DO LISTEN.
And untold EVIL has happened.

The WORLD is now inhabited by the devil and his minions.

We are in the era, the era of the Beast....

The coming of the last days and nights, the end where all
time, as we know it shall cease.

Take care in what you think and wish for, trouble you might
get. After the disappearance of many, shall be confusion,
chaos, and fret.

The rising of a liar, whom many will believe.
The beginning of trial by fire and martyrdom to leave.

Pray for the rapture and your space to be reserved.
Watch the signs of tomorrow, look out for all the curves.

The slate has already been issued,
after the liar comes the mark; acceptance of this will burn you,
tough in the devil's world, you will live.

But in the end comes final judgement and the mark will be regarded
and the highest sin.

So watch out for all the signs young sheep, don't fall in love with
sleep. The devil is here, forever on the creep.

And it is you that he's after.

Rise up and challenge him to his face, smash his plans with laughter.

Pledge your allegiance to God, the one and only true master.

Pick up the Phone

Don't be a bitch
pick up your phone.

You could have won
money, maybe a ton.

A million bucks to
buy a billion fucks
all while sitting at home.

Don't be a coward
hiding from bad news.

Don't be a snob
or a piss poor excuse
for a low-life human
waiting to get robbed.

You bought the fucking
thing, to keep upon your
hip.

The phone mainly works
when closest to your lips.

So, don't be a fucked up
lil' bitch

Answer your mother
fucking phone.

"Pansy-ass posing punk wit-iz pussy posse all waitin to get policed da fuk'up"

The Psalm of the Devil

Where was she when time was one ?
When the threads of the earth had not been spun,
To do these things that have been done;
In her days under the sun.

Where was she when God begun,
The wondrous miracles of the sun ?
And caused the earth not to falter,
For yet in his head was her laughter.

Yes, her plans from head to toe.
The very being of her soul.
Her dreams, her thoughts, desires and goals.
Even the feebleness of her human soul;
To grace her period of time.

Where was she ? In his mind.
Where great beasts were formed to rule time.
And power beyond were given to all,
The creations many; big and small.

And true, he created all. You and me.
Yet do we care, or do we see,
with all his power in heaven he be;
the tears he cries for you and me,
by our actions in the sun ?

Oh where ? Where can we run,
from one who knows all, to all, that we've done ?
To him, to her, to everyone we see;
The Archangel will say, *"Come to me."*

I'll give you all,
I'll make you well,
I'll give you riches,
I'll give you powers,
I will fulfill your lusts.

Listen to me until your days of dust.

For in true, I know as well,
By his right hand I sat, until I fell.

But come to me, come to my home,
come to hell.

For there, I shall not rule you;
but forsake you I have, deceive you I will.
For I have come to destroy, steal, and kill.

All.

Everyone in my sight;
all wielded by his might.
For hated by me, is he, the Father of us all,
You and me.

Well!

I guess it's too late for you can tell,
who I am, the Ruler of Hell.

Your sworn enemy who you have not seen;
the Destroyer of all your dreams.
The Herald of Pain, the Wielder of the sword, Death.
I'll keep you down until your very last breath.

Why ?

Because I need you.

What can be done to escape me ?

Read.

The speared tip of a godly tongue
shall render me undone.

For from you I shall flee,
For cowardice is in me.

Even I am scared, my own death is at hand.
One thousand years suffering after the destruction
of all land.

And locked away from golden haze,
the Glory of Heaven; in a burning blaze,
I will sit; -- but alone, I will not be.

I'll take your Mother, Daughter, Father or Son,
Before time is done, for over some:
I have already won.

How did I come ?
As a Man, Woman, Lust, Desire or a Quirk
To you, I came, your soul I jerked.

But why be angry ?
Why be mad ?

You let me in and left God sad
with your own actions insane.

So where will she be,
When Jesus comes to take her from me,
and those with him to reign ?

I know not,
nor care not,
for until that day I'll cause all pain.

I'll plague her thoughts,
Torment her soul
rip her mind,
and in time - woo her.

For I despise all who ascend higher
and leave me here to burn in fire.

Where will you be,
by your actions,

When God comes to destroy me ?

Snob gets the whip

I should break your fucking nose
Just so you'd lose your direction.

I should doink in your eyeballs,
just to invert your corrupted vision.

I should sew your mouth shut,
just to show you that I could.

I should pull your fucking teeth
out, so you'd have to slurp your
fuckin food.

You snooty lil' fag-ass bastard bitch
you're about to get the whip !

Cut your fucking back to ribbons,
open your ass, so your blood the
leather will sip.

Keep it up you highbrow faggot,
Keep acting like you don't fucking
bleed and god dam –
see what happens.

I'll crush your fucking knee caps,
so you could only crawl in a circle.

Snatch your nuts from between your
legs, have you talking like Steve Urkle.

Fuck up your windpipe, so much,
you'll breathe like a piece-of-shit fish.

Make it so god dam dark in your life,
sunlight your ass would miss.

And all this shit –
I'll do on a nice, breezy god dam Tuesday.

So, imagine what it'd be like,
when it rains?

Talking Heads

Don't you hate it when
people are just talking?

And spittle is flying
from their mouths
like the shit they
always seem to say.

Don't you know that
life and death, rests in
the power of the tongue.

That's not me saying this,
that dates back to the Bible.

So, who would know, right
from wrong, other than God
who put this whole play into
motion.

And everyone is just reciting
their lines and wasting time,
when the words move in no
direction and rings of untruth.

Too many fucking talking
heads in this world and
not enough action.

Too many bullshit mother
fuckers saying too much
and getting away with
murder of the word.

God damn, where's my trusty
fuckin Louisville Sluggie, cause
there is just too many talking
fucking heads in the world and
it's time to put some lights out.

That I just can't see ...

We were all once alive,
and we thrived, in our moment of time,
and we played and had our fun,
under the cherry-pecan sun.

We worked, we loved, we lost,
we counted costs and we grew
from seeds to sinew, and in all
measures in between.

So, not me, the typical,
I find nothing so whimsical,
but sit amused by the bemusement
of waywardness and law, the fractal
shadows of emptiness with
ignorance equaling loneliness.

I know, I sound like a broken CD,
records skipped, but at least CD's
are much more clear, you can tell from
my rant, that I just want to get the fuck
outta here, cause like Hendricks said,
"Life is but a joke."

Don't say any corny shit about me,
like I was a shining star who burnt out
too fast, or God needed me elsewhere.

Fuck you and him, we are all here on
our own dime, trying to make them into
quarters.

I'm just tired man, can't you hear?
But my words fall into a black hole,
so you can't.

And if I fall off the face of the earth,
then what would you care, from this
tempered rant?

Just be like the rest and call me crazy,
call me stupid, call me an Orangutan in
heat, call it indifferent, or tell me you'll
call me, then don't call me at all. (normal)

You'll show me where I rank in your
world really easy.

Funny how we all came here to be alive,
excited like pups, then ended up, walking
around dead from the neck up.

So, what the fuck,
if I'm gone,
I'll see you again,

maybe -

But, maybe is a whole other world,
and a whole other poem,
and a whole other story,
and a whole other reality,
that I just can't see.

Post Script:

"Oh Lord, why do the wicked prosper?"

(Habakkuk 1.13, Jeremiah 12.1)

Answer-

*"Because, unlike the saintly, the wicked
will get off of their asses and do shit !"*

What does it matter

No one has a soul any more.
I search around in the dark
reaching and clawing for
the door.

It's time for me to leave now.
It's time for me to go home.

I'm not invited to this feast,
of lies, and hatred and deceit.

I'm not part of this journey into
misery.

I don't do well when I see things
that float by and then disintegrate
before my very eyes.

I shudder when I watch beauty
effortlessly destroy itself.
And love is flushed down to the
sea.

I joke that the fish all have my
dreams, but those ugly things
only love one another in their
stomachs in a feeding frenzy.

I query and wonder and ponder,
what I can do, where I can go,
what I can buy to make my life
go by.

No one cares about the blackened
candle, no one misses, he, the sad
writer, everyone eventually forgets
the dead friend.

No one cares when you say, I will
stand with you to the very end.

That's just a lie in their eyes.
And what do you really want?

We are all in it for ourselves,
we will fuck or steal or kill or rape,
to get by in the time we have.

What an evil world, so full of excuses.
What a place where the surface is only
good, and true breadth of meaning,
means nothing.

Where it's like playing pin the donkey on
the tail, only the beast hasn't stop spinning
and innocence is ignored, disregarded to
fend for itself, until it ain't so innocent
no more.

The corruptive mar of reason.
Where no loving words can pierce.
No pain is resounded and no amount
of closeness can be located.

We are flea bitten and dirty, though
we prance about as if we were clean.
Souls black as abyss, and full of the
ravenous monsters which
plague the deep.

With teeth sharp as stilettos, and skin
as oily as sweat. Eyes brash with vile,
temper-mental reasoning guided from
self-propelled knowledge and not the
true gift of the common sense world.

A place where an ounce of love dries
up and dies like a snowflake under a
blowtorch, because we laugh and scorn
and toss and beat and kick and spit the
living shit out of it, when it has clawed
at the fact that it had value and wanted
to desperately manifest.

We are all riding on a ship fools.

And maybe deserve the hatred fates
which kindredly befall us.

No one is serious,
no one is precious,
so no one is meant for us.

So, really – what does it matter.
In ponderance – what does it matter.

I'm just a stupid lost soul like any other.

And I'm searching for the bottle to crawl
back into and be no more.

Who deserves a bullet

Fuck It –
I'll tell ya,
cause I'm like that
and I'm strapped -
ready to deliver.

If when you lose your job
and shiver, I understand.

While on this world,
you got to work if you're a
man, and it's worse if you
have mouths to feed,

while you went to work and did
everything you could,

some low level, sub-psychological,
egotistical asshole Manager,
wants to take your dinner –
This nigger, deserves the
144 grain to the groin,
before you close his eyes
wide open.

Fuck him.

He wants you to be in the poorhouse,
by taking your source - of comfort in
your life, because of whatever shit.
Put your deuce in his bit and rid the
nigger of his wig.

Next up, is the pompous shopping
bitch, who wants you to buzz around
her flythie ass, listening to her bullshit
about Neiman Marcus or spinning class.
-- low cut V-neck shirts, grape fruit
hanging like they are screaming to be
free massaged right there on the tree –
then

the hoe wants to talk about her boyfriend.

Time for this bitch's end – to a cavernous
body bag and a bagpipe funeral
– shoot
the bitch in her sweater kitten and watch
the milk spill next to her fucking brains.
Then, if there's enough time left,
rape the hoe
before she turns cold.

Lastly –
Listen, I ain't no cop.
Why? Cause maybe yo mama
deserve to die. Don't ask me sheitzie

When a man got a good woman,
and abuses her, then she's walking
around on the street, turning tricks
to anyone she meets, and yet, she
was a good woman, who would
cook, and clean and give him kids,
this nigga needs a plug to the cray,
and fuck up his grey – cause that
shit is the beginning of poison for
the rest of the planet; when I man,
can't seem to even find a good woman,
who the Bible says is worth her
weight in gold. *(Pv 31:10)*

So, anyone who destroys a good woman's
heart, mos-def, needs a gun-barrel up his
ass, or maybe a fist, or his nuts stomped
to the size of puffer fish.

Fuck – I'm just tired of stupid insane
shit on Planet Wrong, maybe we
all need to take one to the head.

27

The Voice of my own thinking...

comes on sometimes
like wind breaking

and
can be
as invasive

as

a knife
in the gut

sometimes
I wish
and
often are
those times

that
my mind

would
just

shut

the

fuck

up

Writing en la Gulag

Me and my American complaints
without restraint
bitch-bitch-bitch about
the 1000 count sheets
making me itch

or one of my three cars - not starting
the toast being lightly-browned
god dam it – I stubbed a toe
trying to fix a backed up
toilet bowl – won't mention
how (– you get the drift...)
too much o'dat good ole'
filet mignon ... son

here I am miffed
in my one-man-man-castle
writing my modern-day
epistle of
existence in blessed grace

oh America, the beautiful...
America the free...
America for all – you and more so
for me...

with all our property and technology
dishwashers that walk the dog
jobs by the gobs
and money locked away in dark
rooms (*buu-uu—ha-ha-ha-haaaaaa*)
laughter of a mad man

as I sit in trying to scan to see --
if my neighbor covets me

or if it should be,
vice-versa-like-wise

look, not tryna be a smart-ass

I just lost
the most important
thing besides my sanity
and my
just over broke luxury

she was my queen bee

now – I'm looking at all the
clutter before me and out
the window at the here after

… here I am …
writing en la Gulag
a comfy prison
a natural disaster

feeling like I've painted
myself into a red corner
and sold my shoes, due,
to amputated feet

it'll be a feat for me to get
over this solitary in any
sort of solitude with an
bit of solace

yea – I'm feeling grim

THE GRAY
(brought to you by…)

Bespoke Rules of Engagement

Isn't it so funny, though I've arrived at an age where anything seldom is
and I've reached a stage in life where some haven't, can't, won't – some
desire, passed and others still towards aspire.

Last time I checked, I'm still about a million miles off course so living in
Rome (*for quite some time*;) doing as the Romans do is quite for fools.

Escape-witness is futile to the masses droned away in slumber, pennie-
ander, none are awake, and I am eluded by the one and only, true you.

It's funny, concerning and at the same moment troublingly-liberating
how the balance of how much one can learn, earn, make or obtain has
very little in common twain with actual real gain or even good-brains.

Gain in applicable knowledge, reliable wisdom, unshakable decision
making capability, stalwartness of heart or cement of character; in
modern age, people appear white-washed as ever with a yellow
streak

no real crème risen to the top in the ice cream cone if you know what I
mean.

Keurig's broken with no coffee to wake up and smell. I'll forget dreams
that's a whole different stage of frequency and blasted to torturous hell.

observation
retention
of revelation
on a situation
of mitigation
causes remediation
to any sort
of redemption

en Biblical terms – repentance

no travelling past the dividing line of life,
looking around-forward-back-to and through

It's funny to witness people who never once budge in shedding the
skin of childish whims so it clings to them like a sort of itchy old suit
of graham crackers

which creeks and flakes at each and every step and turns to leave
a detectible trail wherever they might roam – I'm probably in this
same category of sorts, so – who am I to point out the sty in your
eyes as the lengthy beam careens from my own.

Others' are still clothed, though stark naked, wearing clothes akin to
the foolish Emperor in the child's story a light fabric, sheer and airy

leaving nothing to the imagination of within any mental range

Equations – I once illustrated, lessons recently in my own garden of pain.

How, a man might try to change a woman's plans with his demands or
worse, his hands; not me on the latter too old for that but my heart knows
fully well this loss.

The only thing (*I can only imagine,*) a woman may respond to is openness,
consistency, understanding and love. Is that caboose a seemingly lost
commodity or cause--, maybe for me only.

Long ago it was equated to me that women are like sands at the beach,
where the residue of a scooped up handful as it sifts through your fingers
in the final stage is what you will get, be so happy, there is no having it all.

Do something else, show anything else and they more than likely will
be in the process of hating you while loving you – leaving you or cheating
on you while killing you or all of the previous in secession.

Yes, fire exists even within the meekest and tamest beauty – fire-ice
steel and feathers, co-reside, and one can burn or freeze just as well
as the other can comfort or kill, or all at the same.

Men are lost when the fire is extinguished from their eyes as dreams
are stomped out by the corporate footprints with world-sized shoes,
expressive rules and too much TV.

You think Lebron James gives a fuck about you, that shit is lame and funny.

It's not the men's faults, rather, the men before him and the men before
them and the men before them – who failed to look farther down the far
and rusty pipeline to see just who

… they might be destroying.

The Bottom

Did you truly think I'd stay
    on the bottom?

Did you really think, I would, forever
    remain down?

When in my darkest hours of fretting my greatest fears
    and lonely in my tears,
        it so much seemed,
    I would drown.

I've went straight down to the bottom
    Hit the bottom so hard,

Been covered in my bruises and accepted
    the welts of my scars.

And now, humbly, shuffle on.

For in my broken woes,
    A true power within me rose,

And now it goes, to show, the display of
    my inner ambitions.

For God stretched out his hand,
    and on his strength I stand,

For he lifted me as Man,
    from that position.

My improvement, lacks regret,
    My motives pure as snow,

The keys to my soul's future I possess,
    with less stress and no duress.

I seek only one now to impress,

And that's me.

The Dream Comes...

and then it evaporates,
leaving us to ask, ponder,
wonder and to equate

a time of when or where to pick
a date, for a time and chance on
romance.

As in a nightmare, there is fear.

Seasons of not knowing,
trying and reaching; there
seems to be something so
distracting – and maybe
misleading. Even fleeting.

As long as we are caring
sharing and talking, then
we can be loving, even in
the moments we have
before love.

And after the conversations
and the connections, when we
are so immersed in affection -

it is then
and there

in the
when

and
in
the
where

that

the

Dream

finally comes…

36

Fragile Balances

How could it be
that we
can sometimes see
such beauty
then mix it with envy,
the good fortunes of
family
or love
or any blessing from above

How can we entertain
such thoughts –
of hate
or deception
or murder

In a place of children's laughter,
and the suns' beauty clear rays
of a bright new day

When so much good is laying
asleep at our fingertips, and
only requires a gentle caress
to wake it patiently and lovingly up.

How do the old die lonely
Why does a woman corrupt
her beauty

Why does a child who laughed
in growing up, turn out to hate their life

Why does the innocent, painfully die

Is it us – or them – or me
society
Or just my stupid pen –
again?

My tears bubble up, as I sketch
with words in the wind.

My thoughts create your thinking
maybe, in courses of flashing visions

Where in a world away from you
relaxing, I could be rotting,
for my time had eventually come.

No – life is never done

and never fooled, for there is
nothing new under the sun.

But things exist in these
fragile balances.

Minor occurrences which may
lead to major victories.

Huge successes which carve trails
of traumatic pitfalls and defeats of
despair with no ability to repair.

All things hinge, on so fine-a-thin
razor blade's edge, cantilevered ledge,
that in comparison provides the support
in likened effect, of a steel girder.

And then I think
Just how much I loved her.

The speak came after a
week of searching for the
right words to say.

Maybe, it just wasn't the time –
Or I wasn't enough –
The balance wasn't right,
or she wasn't the one for me.
Fragile balances don't always
work in favor of feeling or desires.

They balance - remember?

Lessons.   Too many.

Every opportunity,
to gain a widget of knowledge
strain to remain on the
cusp, in a leading-edge of understanding –

My tears pour internal,
like a salt-warm waterfall.

Oh my gall,
to Love Her

Requiring such a fine imbalance
of timing
like our lives entwining,
in a friendly game of
cold war, tug-o-war.

And as usual,
shit I lose.

But, just because my battles
are fought –
and my sanity frays due
to the mental ground that
was given up –

Whilst I look across to
a happy family unit,
at play without a care
in the world,
on a shimmering, sunny,
sandy, private beach –

On a bright clear day –

I have to be realistic to ask myself –

Is everyone fighting?
Or struggling?

losing?
Or dying?

Just like lonesome old me?

no not even close

Those are the fine
fragile balances of life

that are constantly working –

and that only,

I might be missing.

Galvanized and given the keys...

I don't really know what happened
knocked unconscious and woke up a whole new person

feral strong, peregrine aperture, in-depth focused far beyond
recognition
- a resurrected wretch from utter perdition

where from did this subzero in-human ability surface
this amass of armor plating
sterner compelled reasoning
nil passes the vision of kaleidoscopic-panoramic-ommatidia

loving her for a torrid season gave birth to a mutated-strength
sans her presence by absentia

fully aware, I was able to take advantage
and now understood the comic-book hero who couldn't be bought
nor compromise en leveraged-against mentality

described; my life – swimming in the ocean without a boat,
paddling till every stroke was a sinew strain against mile-high waves
amid lactic acid muscle drain

while is this midst, the liquid turns to gasoline; my eyes burn
my skin chaffs – and everything I see is now violently set ablaze

I revel in being too old for propositions
too far gone to imagine or hope on an angel, else I can be lifted
out of the notion that we are all extremely self-fish deities
unto our own slimy miniscule scales

but what this little experiment did successfully do
was surgically remove my heart confusions,
found all the correct margins
and excised the cancer

I'm free of injury yet restrain myself to injure (*as best I can...*)

It's a snorked, half-laugh with snot and spittle as someone else
might clumsily stumble over toes throughout their woes –
I'm not trying to laugh or be mean

it just helps to have steel-toed shit kicker, hip-high boots, in order
to wade through all the bullshit someone will, warm, hand to you

painful and dreadful, so internally doubtful at that time,
but now I can't thank her enough

Dandy – dam, I purely thought you were a fucking Demon –
a Succubus from hell no less; and maybe you are – all I know is,
I love the lessons that you taught me, ha! – *yeah now…*
going through them was a calloused-roughened bitch

cause you set me free to hover high above the blackened cumulous
clouds to witness how dark the rest of the world appears under them

no changing that – plenty tried and died
not in my control and wouldn't want it if handed a golden key
where to go now, now that I'm given this *"altitu-ative"*- attitude

still working on that
having better vision, doesn't provide all the readymade answers
but it's a start

if everyone could see, maybe what a better, practical world

Naaa

Every man is afloat, in his own personal life preserver and there's
never near a ship in sight – as long as I got mine's - *(right?)*

I guess, self-fish living is best,
I mean, heck – we all looted the village who once raised the child

No one should wonder about the incarceration rates, that stemmed
from that one lone dumbass, no one should care about – the crazy
loser who dons a mask after writing a manifesto and relieves a little
bit of pent up pain *(ooops,)* … I once explained

it's the Crystal Castles that we all build in our heads – in our hearts
and sometimes in our minds, those must often be smashed to truly
show and know that – *(I imagine…)* necessity of lessons in that…

we are all not in control –

that the two sides to any spectrum are much more closer than anyone
could ever believe and often touch at moments of grandeur, doubt,
next steps, routinely…(*day/night, wealth/poverty, love,thin-line,hate.*)

and here – if I were God or even a tenth his size and power
be jealous that someone did it without me
and maybe find glory and glee
in watching their dominoes fall down

I know, where's the balance in this, right

I was trying to provide a story to educate, mitigate and predicate
but I'm only good at the subjugate part

I'm not one to really ever listen to even my own preaching,
(*common to give great advice but never receive it,*)
nor use the keys well that I were given,

though water and fire proof,
they seem to fit no lock at all that I can find

I'm just another passing vapor in

with another kind of

fractal opinion

That Great Plate of Pain …

Did you know that the soul suffers stains?
Stains from remorse, regret, hurts, anger,
these elements, the meat-slicer of existence
and provides feed for the trough of despair.

No matter your level, status, degree, or
breed, all have dined in this capacity.

Tortuous visions from memory
and glancing blows in ebb numbing woes.

This dish, I dismiss, the Great plate of Pain.

Laden with inconsistency, infidelity,
indifference and individuality, lots of in's, including insane.

For think of the phrases, in trouble, in denial, in doubt,
in the hospital, all pitfalls to this soup called life.

Do we desire this meal, *(hardly)*
this hunger producing diet of
thorns, beetles and needles, beats Keto like Kato easily.

Is it an automatic, autonomic, autopilot to an anonymous
situation; an asynchronous antithesis to seeking happiness.

Who wants to hurt? In a world where trouble can be
found at the very next turn or off-ramp?

Who wants to fight, when it could mean dying and never
loving again?

What idiot poisoned loving in the first place with diseases,
deception and price tags? Was it Satan? What a guy.

I'm tired, I've said this before in other things I've written,
but it's been ten years now. And the only thing that comes
to mind is when I held a gun to my head at nineteen.

The rouge silence that crept in,
the demons wriggling in the wind
waiting for me to finally fall.

As you can tell, our hero still exists,
but now it been nearly fifteen years since
ten and I can only say,
I wish there were another way to
live another fucking fifteen.

I've had friends die before me,
placed in miniscule graves
amongst the common, forgive me.

Because these people were not common,
they befriended me,
and that's extraordinary.

As I sit, I'm in love again, with a girl who's hard to get.

I always thought hard to get women weren't worth the
trouble, but she is, because she represents the future.
Not mine, mind you, but the future of humanity.
(*Could never lump her into MANkind.*)

I've just lost a girlfriend who loved me very much and all
I can say is good luck.

I was married to the woman of my dreams for a season
and now I can say, I still love her, but what doesn't
work or doesn't fit, just doesn't like too small shoes.

Sorry, I've run out of steam, for the poetry thing. (*oh, there it goes*)
And that Great plate of Pain is just a mind game, one that brings
shame, by second nature.

Well, if you've read through the course of this semi-poetic verse,
all I can really say, is thanks for eating the potatoes.

Kill Cupid

lil ma'aa fuckin stupid--
-- arrows n' shit --

sure, feels nice when it
works out, no doubts
and she's in your corner;
or he, def' not sayin' U ladies don't have
problems cause man
- I've seen

take-this-fuk'n-shit
you "tra-la-la-in" lil
fuk'n bitch with nuthin'
better to do than with
your time screw and
arrows shoot into you

eva been shot wivf'a
real fuk'n arrow mang?

Only famous person I
know (heard of) lived
with one suck right
below his right eye –

Lucky his ass was da
King, so no one could
talk mess about his
face

Cupid need all dem arrows
blown-up-his-asshol' mang

tired of try'na do shit
and when you try'na
concentrate and get
somewhere and try'na
not care – there he
is standing there with
a lil bitch-ass grin

zoom – haaaaw shit
who was that chick
that just walked by?

Betta clean up yo
vernacular son
or dem tears will
Shirley come

sheeeet, maybe
it's just me
and my old-ass-age

I be seeing these
broke young cats
with some beautiful
young women and
I hafta wonder –
how does that happen?

Or women who want to
claim abuse and then
screw you for the
proverbial
"cock in the bottle,"

I mean, if you hafta
cheat with me, then,
 – times are hard
and so was I

back to Cupid – that
simp – mutha fukkin
limpin-pimp with a quiver

should find where he
lay his head at 'nd twiss
his fuck'n cap back

Now I sound like
I'm from NWA

It's just my bad luck
and I'm so stuck, fulla
bleeding holes from
that butthole

nigga-Fuk Cupid

KNIFE BLADE

Thin and strong

serrated and long

a flash from your side means death

a whisper in the wind

you cut while
I sing,

my trusty
stainless kitchen help

Go figure.

Love is like…

an open window
a beautiful hole that
exposes your soul.

It's sunny, airy, breezy
and light
allows in fresh air
and cricket sounds
at night.

It makes you feel safe
and secure knowing
now an exit exists
if you can't get through
the door.

Bird songs sound clearer
windows endear a house
to be brighter and cheerier

But – when your love is
damaged and your window
is shattered-

Your safety feels compromised
The glass now jagged,
and cuts like razors

Cold air billows throughout
your home and rain blows
into-on anything that means
something to you and makes
everything feel like nothing.

You spend much more time looking
wondering-thinking and wishing
that it was fixed. And it makes
you feel pissed because of the
damage and the time and effort
it will take to get over the intrusion.

You're left with so much frustration
while the person who pitched the
rock, just simply walks away.

One Chance

Is all anyone, in anything can ever hope for really
a chance to use your gifts, apply your talents, deliver all your love
all of the above to get past that seemingly locked door

there can be a hundred no's – a thousand maybe's – a million missed
calls – a billion strikes or a quintillion passed away; but, oh that one
chance

makes all that defeat so sweet

that one chance, feels like a window installed in a prison wall
that one chance, feels like a gulp of air as in when you're drowning
or better yet, on the horizon, a ship and some hot chocolate for a long
ride home

Home – such a good feeling.
safety – tranquility – solace, maybe a special person there who gave
you that one chance to love them and them, you (not just co-exist.)

One chance.

Any poor person, just needs one to prove themselves
Any broken hearted person needs to change their perspective

One chance

is the doorknob to the dimension of *"IF,"*

But that one chance usually seems so well hidden and far, far away
a difficult struggle to obtain when sogged with rain and it's actually
a lighting storm

crossroads

because I love the most awesome person right now and I write this
for her in absentia; she gave me a very small chance – kinda like, a
starter chance for the minor leagues, ya know, not a full chance at
all

No one ever said those one chances weren't sometimes strange
difficult or scary and I want her to know, I understand where you
are – but definitely not how you got there

I did see your needs and wanted to fulfill them
I did hear your fears and was there to silence them
I did know what was important to you
and it was double-important to me

I would never ask you to leave stability for instability
I am and always will be holding my own with groans

I loved you – (the real you)
I experienced you – (a taste)
and can't get the flavor out of my mind

I'm only this smart to know that with you –
all I ever needed or could have ever hoped for

was one real chance

and not something that left me internally wondering

what was that all ever really about

One Seat Theater
(Memory outweighs Words)

What does anyone truly remember
sounds, imagery, PTSD

still pictures or cut scenes from things
that made us happy or may have been
traumatic

sights and decibels starburst to the fore
front of our frontal lobes with music if
it matches said moment

memories are so much heavier than
words

words can be misinterpreted or even
forgotten but the beauty of scenery
is relived in pop-flash crescendos of
the past

all the feelings are there, all the emotions
the hormonal whirlwinds that made your
inner walls feel coated with drunken ants
gingerly stepping along the highway of your
nervous esophagus and tip-toing through
the verticals of a joy filled heart

only a person can know how these revisits
can make them feel – like translucent gold
only they or we individually can go back in
time and see the faces and relive the words
that make us cry or spurned them to action
- or made them a hero

poured enchantment upon their being
gave them the loving eyes of one other
soul towards them (us) that made us (them)
wonder how could luck be so blind to spend
this endless amount of time with who they were

memories are so much heavier than words
and the light in surfacing from this theater
- brings back the coldest of realities

Planet Wrong

Ho my God, what's going on?
Way things happen, Planet Earth should be titled, Planet Wrong.

O.k. I know, you've read a lot; -- A lot of my bitching, (*so far…*)
But on this particular subject you know I've been dying and itching,
to get to the heart of the matter so all can understand.

Man,

You profess love for a woman and she says no.
Selective I guess wreaks havoc within your soul.

Like scraping out your being with a dull ice cream scoop, then
handing it to you and telling you, "now go outside and play."

Your guts are dangling from threads, and the pain won't seem to end.
You fight hard to make amends--,
Against her well placed walls, iron words and hard (but still beautiful)
eyes.
Me, she must despise – you wonder, through the disaster, as your
desire seems to thrash about within you, as if drowning in a pool.

Then she sits with losers and casts her precious warmth to ominous fools.
Who'll use it, abuse it and over her rule, or possibly leave her
crying and bitter in a place where you would have guarded with
your very life.

The strife, the strife …

That's caused in this thought, this emotion, this actions, this anti-
reasonable un-navigational journey into crushed hearts, bruised plans
and wounds to lick for extended periods of time.

When will the pain cease in the mind,
Of the visuals of her walking by, hair blowing in the breeze,
not a care in the world.

-- about you anyway, the jilted reject.

But this space is so small, so personally awful.

Planet Wrong, on a grander scale, is a long, unworthy tale,

Think of traffic, who's in the front?

Think of working, a white-collar, high dollar crime perpetrated against man, for the weather man says, it'll be a great day outside, but you're stuck in an office, so how the hell would you really know, driving in traffic – I suppose…

Think of where all the departed lovers go, or the Fathers who walk away from their crying children for another woman. Self-fishness.

Think of the boastful, their inflated pride, their boisterous egos and in control ids. What is this a Psychology lesson? I hate Psychology.

Man's attempt to neatly package life in pretty little removal, re-sealable, freezer proof envelopes.

Pavlov's Dogs, what a find, starve anything to death and mind fuck it while hungry, I'd salivate too.

Where am I going with this you wonder?

as you can tell, as of late, my banter,
has been somewhat fodder,
because you know I'm better with the letter,
than most others,

but remember,
as in the playing of any off key song ….

I sit and write -

on Planet Wrong.

Sandstorm

makes you cry
whips stingingly-violent
with painful accuracy
against the cover of
your face

narrows your vision
invades your sinuses
chokes off your
airway so your life
support, fuels short

dry throat parched
muscles strain
against the quicksand
drain sometimes
pulling you
under
the
tundra

crunch between your teeth
voices *"this is no beach,"*

pesky gnats make a nest
right inside your nostrils
and drink the tears from
the sides of your eyes

swallowing feels like a Bic
lighter was clicked on the
under and back of your
soft palette making breathing
a wheezing chore indeed

just a tiny uncomfortable
part

of fighting a distant distal
war

SEX

Desirable
Obsessive
Now!
Tangible

Curious
Harrowing
Ambrosial
Savory
Ecstatic

Innovative
Too much, never enough.

xve

Me a perv?

Put a Smile on your face...

(do *something today* ...)

No Matter What It Costs
No Matter What It Takes
Do Something TODAY
That Puts A Smile On Your Face !

Because throughout this so called
"human race" someone is racing
at a steady pace to take your place

without regard of your feelings
and at the expense of the true
You

Is being self-fish a popular virtue
certainly not-well untrue

Because we come here by self
we grow and learn with minimal help
and no matter how many fill the room
you are the one sole maybe dying

so enough trying
in being so pleasing and appeasing
to those who leech off your inner
goodness – then go on to foolishness;
leaving you standing with the mop
to sop up your tears

lean your complaints up against moments
of ecstasy you create because the morning
dawn one day may never turn to
evening shade

Reach for what you need.
Sample every peach and toss the
stupid seed !

Plant, plant, plant but never grow.

because in the end my friend
good and bad times both end
so at least build great memories
to take with you as you
go

Static

In the old days – was the broadcast from
midnight to six-thirty

Fuzzy snow and one horridly, grating TV noise;
it was working fine, just a case of lights on and
no one at home

Drag your feet across the floor
touch the knob of the door
and get that angry little zap –

Dry cotton with polyester
no Bounce to try to sequester
and after – all kinds of shit
will stick to your chest

Static, isn't it lovely
scientific glue of sorts
repellant in other ways

like – talk to someone
talk with someone
or talk at someone

sounds similar

but if you're smart enough after living
through these three – you might agree

static for we, is when I believe I have
said everything I can just right
illustrated all possible angles and
protracted as many reasons to a fault

fought, pulled, loved, hurt, cried and
died with every beat of my confused
heart

and the mess just gets ignored
twisted – not understood or well-received

snow blind to words, gaggled with ignorance

I don't think there is more to say on this topic
(Static could also just be what's in my own head...)

58

That I just can't see ...

We were all once alive,
and we thrived, in our moment of time,
and we played and had our fun,
under the cherry-pecan sun.

We worked, we loved, we lost,
we counted costs and we grew
from seeds to sinew, and in all
measures in between.

So, not me, the typical,
I find nothing so whimsical,
but sit amused by the bemusement
of waywardness and law, the fractal
shadows of emptiness with
ignorance equaling loneliness.

I know, I sound like a broken CD,
records skipped, but at least CD's
are much more clear, you can tell from
my rant, that I just want to get the fuck
outta here, cause like Hendricks said,
"Life is but a joke."

Don't say any corny shit about me,
like I was a shining star who burnt out
too fast, or God needed me elsewhere.

Fuck you and him, we are all here on
our own dime, trying to make them into
quarters.

I'm just tired man, can't you hear?
But my words fall into a black hole,
so you can't.

And if I fall off the face of the earth,
then what would you care, from this
tempered rant?

Just be like the rest and call me crazy,
call me stupid, call me an Orangutan in
heat, call it indifferent, or tell me you'll
call me, then don't call me at all. (normal)

You'll show me where I rank in your
world real easy.

Funny how we all came here to be alive,
excited like pups, then ended up, walking
around dead from the neck up.

So, what the fuck,
if I'm gone,
I'll see you again,

maybe -

But, maybe is a whole other world,
and a whole other poem,
and a whole other story,
and a whole other reality,
that I just can't see.

What does it matter

No one has a soul any more.
I search around in the dark
reaching and clawing for
the door.

It's time for me to leave now.
It's time for me to go home.

I'm not invited to this feast,
of lies, and hatred and deceit.

I'm not part of this journey into
misery.

I don't do well when I see things
that float by and then disintegrate
before my very eyes.

I shudder when I watch beauty
effortlessly destroy itself.
And love is flushed down to the
sea.

I joke that the fish all have my
dreams, but those ugly things
only love one another in their
stomachs in a feeding frenzy.

I query and wonder and ponder,
what I can do, where I can go,
what I can buy to make my life
go by.

No one cares about the blackened
candle, no one misses, he, the sad
writer, everyone eventually forgets
the dead friend.

No one cares when you say, I will
stand with you to the very end.

That's just a lie in their eyes.
And what do you really want?

We are all in it for ourselves,
we will fuck or steal or kill or rape,
to get by in the time we have.

What an evil world, so full of excuses.
What a place where the surface is only
good, and true breadth of meaning,
means nothing.

Where it's like playing pin the donkey on
the tail, only the beast hasn't stop spinning
and innocence is ignored, disregarded to
fend for itself, until it ain't so innocent
no more.

The corruptive mar of reason.
Where no loving words can pierce.
No pain is resounded and no amount
of closeness can be located.

We are flea bitten and dirty, though
we prance about as if we were clean.
Souls black as abyss, and full of the
ravenous monsters which
plague the deep.

With teeth sharp as stilettos, and skin
as oily as sweat. Eyes brash with vile,
temper-mental reasoning guided from
self-propelled knowledge and not the
true gift of the common sense world.

A place where an ounce of love dries
up and dies like a snowflake under a
blowtorch, because we laugh and scorn
and toss and beat and kick and spit the
living shit out of it, when it has clawed
at the fact that it had value and wanted
to desperately manifest.

We are all riding on a ship fools.

And maybe deserve the hatred fates
which kindredly befall us.

No one is serious,
no one is precious,
so no one is meant for us.

So, really – what does it matter.
In ponderance – what does it matter.

I'm just a stupid lost soul like any other.

And I'm searching for the bottle to crawl
back into and be no more.

What I wasn't given …

Was a smile.
Or Joy.
Or parents,
or even goals.

What I discovered …
Was a world.
Inside.
On a whole,
and it was cold.

What I had to do …
Was dig.
And fix.
And plant.
And grow.

What I found …
Was my room.
My tools.
To build,
my life.

And I worked …
Alone.
Long.
In silence.
Tireless.

And I built …
A system.
Which works,
for me.
With progress.

What do I have …?
My strength.
My stories.
My emotions.
My loneliness.

Where I am …
Is hunted.
And shunned.
And shamed
And used.

Pelted …
with lies,
with insults,
and injustice,
and rocks,

Through which I stand.
Do I care?

No.

Why should a spirit
care what you think.

When my tears turn to rain drops ...

There's going to come a day,
when all my pain –
gives way,
to a cloud covered sky
within my mind.
A delight to the eyes,
so to speak.

A cleansing wash,
that is defiantly needed.
To scour away, in a given
day, the stains, and scabs,
and scars.

It's not too far.
I can see precipitation.

And in anticipation,
I walk toward the over cast,
because I'm ready to have a
blast.

When my tears turn to rain.
I will reign, in a circle of joy
and not sorrow.

I would have reach that better
tomorrow.

That I lay my head down, while
sleeping in my car, and dreamt
about fourteen years ago.

And the people who have come
and go?

The ones who stood by me?
Intended to harm me?
Dies and cried with me?
and loved me?

They'll all be there in spirit.
And a thought is glowing
from my heart for all, because,
Living Well, is the Best Revenge !

So without further adieu …

Let the rains –

Begin.

When you've lost your way…

anyone can be smart and seem to have it all, then be gay and it wasn't
meant to be that way – yet someone of the opposite sex wants to love
you

one can be gripped in fear; all appears hopeless, a light shines through
the mess, but cautious movements cause more stress – let go
someone might be able to guide you

anger flows immense
focus loss intense
all faith seems incensed
hate is all to vent
regard of the intent
cannot see the gift
of a leader who uplifts
your life of all the strife

- End can be the loss of soul who
once showed dedication

a heart, once young and foolish but full of innocent love
is overturned and long destroyed, like a newborn thrown
to the floor and is now a cripple forever
what do you expect
this son may forget
but the physician's bill will never forgive the damage

As the Bible says, *"Do not feign affection,"* for it hurts someone
who true to you wants to be

if something is destroyed should it ever function again
will it work without repair
who fixes it
if not you

yes, Samaritans do exist, but they only come every other million years

a loss of way is seeing fears and animals as only friends
a loss of way when shown something good believing it bitter for sweet
what a revolting life living door, as when most things get bad, it can
exceedingly get worse

trustworthy - a transparency

deceit cheat lie steal kill hurt, verbs to the actions of the self-fish
make no plans for future plans or for children and not love the person
next to them

patience and understanding are a long cured viruses put out to pasture
only the rats and the dregs of the world, standing on each other's heads
to prop their noses above the water line – before they eventually drown

I (*and trust me, I tried very hard to not put me in this…*)

feel let down

because I can't force my dreams and can't force many or not any
of the things I want – yet find no reserve in giving up,
I never have or would done so, long ago, if not day one

I can't find someone, willing to love me and let me be me;
rolling snake-eyed dice, even betting on ones and still losing

I reach stretch and cannot find an equal; in recalling Ecclesiastes,
"I find one good man in a thousand, but of the women, I find none."

gotta remind myself, I wrote it and read it on Planet Wrong,
taking my lumps and bruises to the head,
to the heart - to the soul - to my will,
but still press forward, hoping to succeed

Even with an innate ability to conjure thought, descriptions, reasons
and describe various seasons

– I can still get snow blinded, disoriented and confused,
as if I have lost my way in an avalanche.

We're all part of the problem

I could just leave the above titled pasted and type… nuff said.
Preachy I know, but we all just aren't that smart, least, I'm not.

I liken myself, in my blessed old-age to the ever lovin' Stout,
sly, a lil cunning, scurrying about – opportunistic, somewhat bombastic
and full of a 'tude of – "no give a ferk."

So, if a stout, halted his touts for two seconds, what would this slippery
little delectable slice of Hawk-lunch meat probably have to say?

"That, we're all part of the problem and no one wants to be the solution."

there was a day – when one man, took on the government, the police,
the neighbors and even and especially the ignorance of those around
him for the betterment of his people
and what did he get

what was his reward, nothing but a bullet to the chest

we celebrate and have holidays and half-off sales for those who gave
a fuck, out their necks stuck and got them chopped clean through.

so in the smallest ways and rightfully so, we remember and try to find
a way that seems right within in our own insecurities, but no advice ever
rings true.

better to lock them up than council them
take from someone to have more for yourself
than build something together and share what you've both grown

Ah – that tiny stout… crouched down, creeping about in the shadows
laughs his head off at us – finally getting down to his level.

he would kick up his heels and diddle-a-fiddle in glee, (*if gifted
opposable thumbs*) at our daily pain and misery

no lesson here
when one tries to talk you out of being a fool
      well, not me
      I mean, no one is listening

I'm too busy fantasizing over the latest gigabit device
being the cool ab-laden guy
getting the girl

or getting to where I wanna go

I'm part of the problem too, at least I certainly and readily do admit
because the solution causes me to think it takes way more than me
to fix and will cost me my dreams

might bring me (more) pain
prompt me to ruin
or forfeit my life

Only God has that big of a bank account to write that kind of check
to repay someone who loses everything and he's great with cows and
chickens, but seems to suck badly with dispensing cash.

my words change no one's thoughts, but my own,
so we are on the stout's turf
and live within his terms

We are all part of the problem
too many – too much – too graphic list –
from plastic to poverty, inflation and economy
rejection, incarceration god, not gonna even try

search your heart, what's left
sear you brain,
to become a seer
for an answer

relive your "devil deeds done in darkness," if you have heart to
there's way more bad than was good done – in honesty …

Oh darn!

there goes my belief
that you are worthy

or have merit

or balance

or justice

Mr. nimble-treble stout

says simply out

be strong and rock on!

YOU TRIED REAL HARD P - II

You tried real hard to tell me I was no good,
You tried real hard to kill my dreams, when I
     was doing things that I thought I should.

You ran out on me, to see the world, and left me
to grow in the backwards care of a monster,

     "You don't go to College, boy, and you'll be a failure !"

Someone is missing, do you give a damn ?
You don't even care.

Family ? *(my ass)*
Did you help me, when I stood and faced
 judgment all alone, out there ?

You had not one thing to do with raising me, and yet,
you blame me and look down your nose for the way I've lived.

 What to my life, have you ever tried to give ?

 What do you know, if anything about me ?
    Anything at all?
Do you know my favorite color ?
food ?
passion ?

You've tried so hard to put me down and gnaw
at my direction.

You're the fool !

I still have time on my side
I still have some cunning
I still have my mind
I dream!

Which is above and beyond the other "dead souls"
you've pushed like maggots crawling out into the world.

I'm your only hope of success in this collection.

And when you're old and grey you may look to me,
            someday,

you might want to pray, -- that I'm in a good mood.

YOU TRIED REAL HARD P – III

You tried real hard, to twist my mind,
    You tried real hard, to test my heart.

You took every kind and loving word I ever gave,
And at one time, threw them in the gutter.

Then you want to be number one in my life,
as soon as we start over ?

Old pains, die hard, sweetheart.

You made me beg to see you, once, on my birthday,
What kind of shit was that ?

You left me standing outside your door, "Go Away"
printed on the mat.

You fought over coming to visit me in the hospital,
and when I was in jail.

And now, because you've changed, so you want all
things to just go swell and well.

    no

Now, I have reserves. I now, don't trust you
It's my turn to do damage
and here your tears go boo-hoo-hoo

"I can't take it anymore." You scream, you say,
"Everyone's treated me badly, I'm a nobody."

    grow up

Give me a break, you're crazy, definitely
I can't help you with your insecurities in your
personality.

And I have no need for a forty-five-year-old baby.

My hat is off to you all,

You all tried so very hard to make me fall,

    and none of you were successful.

THE GOOD

18 inches 1/16 gram

Size and dimensions mean everything.
     They are descriptive, expressive,
and provide tangible structure to the eye,
            for the touch,
            to our perceptions.

Yes, these parameters are extremely important, how you may ask?

18 inches is the distance from the brain to the heart. (Biology 101)
For by naming this measurement, I will describe your most inner being.
The distance, depth, weight and contrast of your human soul.

I could start off by describing the strength, joy and tenderness behind your
youthful, olive eyes and when they change colors based on your mood,
energy or (alcohol) level (whichever was a factor the night before.)

Maybe it could start with the mannequin style beauty in the structure of
your face, the invitation of your smile, the silky, blemish free quality of
your bronzed skin.

(I need to stop the buttering huh?)

I could start with the billion-dollar assembly of your physique, or the arc
and tones of your vocal chords in the missing music sheet that created
your voice.

The serenity of your thoughts, your dreams, your desires –

But, quite honestly – none of the previous described is who you are.
None of these gifts, make up any of us. So I will do my best to make
sense.

Who you are is the struggle between, your head and your heart.
     What you think you want and what you deeply desire.

What you <u>think</u> makes you happy versus what you <u>know</u> makes you
happy.

Very balanced places the brain and the heart,
      Both equally necessary to ensure the physical body survives.

The heart is never fooled in what it desires, but by being innocent in nature, is always fooled by deception.

Notice, the brain gets full, produces headaches, sometimes can't shut down, causing you not to sleep, anxiety, stress, gives out wrong thoughts, whispers things to you that may not be true (my thing). Directs you to places and actions that may appear attractive at the time, but end up in ruin.

Even a sheep loves the rustle of new grass under its' feet, the wind on its' face, while all the birds are telling it that they are his new found friends.

Know what the heart is saying throughout all this?

You shouldn't have left the fence. The shepherd will look for you, and be worried. He will miss you and cry if something truly bad happens to you.

Then again - what does a sheep really know?

But the brain speaks in attractive, singular words:

Freedom, Fun, Excitement, Pleasure, Prestige, Attraction, Delight Ecstasy
…..

All bait to the snares and traps formed from the pressures of life.

The Heart only knows pleasure from one thing – That's Love.
And pain from being hurt,

It doesn't try to weight out costs,   / That's the brain calculating angles
It doesn't try to seek reward,   / That's the brain being greedy
It doesn't what's good or what's not / That's the brain being selective

Funny look at this:

The Brain must THINK while the Heart always KNOWS.

The heart speaks in a language that is seen and not heard. Expressed by emotions and actions and like a backed up sewer pipe, sometimes through words forced from the Brain, when the heart is in control.
(*stiff analogy I know*)

Most sadly, much of the time it is actually the other way around.

The Brain does all the talking, while the Hearts quietly objects.
The Brain speaks in many languages:

English, Korean, French, Japanese, Spanish, Chinese, Italian *(you),*
German, Maori, Hindi, Serf, Farsi, Tagalog to just name a few…

So, WHO WOULD YOU FOLLOW?

Someone who had to think about every decision or step they had to make?
Or someone who already knew?
What, when, where and how they wanted things?

Unfortunately – the heart only knows one language – and that's **Love.**

Often sought out to learn experience and feel, often misinterpreted.
Often denied its' rightful place to be spoken, revealed or accepted.

And the heart continues to hurt in silence.

This cycle describes the waxing and waning of the Human soul.
The war between these two entities is what motivates some, destroys others.

And keeps the world in a constant state of guessing and wondering what's correct and what's not.

The Brain is so easily fooled.

A question was asked of me once, by a very beautiful woman,
"How would she ever know true Love?"

My answer to her was, *"To listen to her Heart.*
It speaks such a simple language."

Oh, and as for the **1/16 gram** –

This is the amount of weight that leaves the body at the exact
moment of Death.

(et. the measured weight of the soul.)

To understand the divulgence of this bit of knowledge;
I would guess is to never feel pressure from anything

– the weight you carry in your being,

truly only weighs

that much.

BLESSED LOVE

Sometimes I think there are ANGELS
that put us in places we don't want to be.

For those are the ones who are special, and that's what I
think happened with you and me.

It occurs each time I look in your eyes; those feelings of
love I could not disguise; and though we are now not
together, I want you to know these feelings are forever.

And maybe, someday, I may have all of that I've dreamed.

Money, fame and lots of things.

But if I could lay them down on the floor, I would hope the
path would lead right back to your door.

Because without you, GOLD is worth DIRT.
And time passes, bringing pain beyond hurt.

Without you the pieces are hard to fit it seems,
and a mind that was full is now tapped of all dreams.

Thoughts continue to roll over in my mind of how it used
to be.

The soft touch,
The passionate kisses,
The beautiful love you made to me.

We were brought together from far across the land,
with an age difference between us; a few years' span.

But we still loved each other just the same.

This was no magical feat;

But, God's, Divine Intervention.

We are two similar persons, yet from totally different nations.

And to anyone in confusion reading this tale:
Don't be afraid to express your love for one who is PALE,
or BLACK, or YELLOW, or GREEN.

Even if your loved one is different from you,
it's only this way as it seems.

We are all people.
Children of light,

With a loving God that has tried to teach us
wrong from right.

To LOVE someone who is different, whether by looks or
difference in age, cannot be a wrong thing.

LOVE is the opposite of HATE,
meaning the opposite of WAR,
meaning the opposite of DESTRUCTION,
meaning the opposite of DEATH.

LOVE whoever you choose, even with your very last breath.

IF,

of your affection, they are truly deserving.

To end this tale, I will finally say,

The world needs more LOVE
and less HURTING.

(you can just hear the pangs of youth in this one...)

The Colors of the Rose

YELLOW stands for FRIENDSHIP,
that, we already have been.

Now comes PINK,
because my INTEREST in you,
is starting to shine in.

Let these figures of delicacy,
bloom,
as a reminder of
me;
in your room.

As RED, for LOVE, opens
to the new day's morning song.

For each new day will come and then the day will soon
be gone.

Let our knowledge of each other grow;
from FRIENDSHIP to
INTEREST to LOVE.

As WHITE, I last will give you,
a symbol of TRUE LOVE.

Let us get to know each other,
better, till the wedding
pictures' pose.

So tells this story,

The colors of the ROSE.

GIVEN TO BE LIVEN

Do you think, life, was given to be liven ?
Nay. It was bought with a price.
For all your silly sins;
died the Lord Jesus Christ.

You say you've heard this all before;
but to how much have you listened ?
Let's play a little game then,
let's call it:
ENVISION.

Could YOU have stood, in the burning desert heat ?
Could YOU have taken lies spoken of you, and your clothes
ripped, down to your feet ?

Could YOU have withstood the whipping from a strongman's arm ?
Could YOU have taken this humiliation ? And through it all,
wished the killer mob, no harm ?

Could YOU have then; since being beaten up;
carried, a HUNDRED POUND CROSS uphill ?

YOU probably haven't eaten ALL DAY, and much blood you have lost.
YOU' RE KICKED in the head, KICKED in the back, and in the ASS.
You're given bitter, gall-water to drink;
how long will this continue,
you ask ?

YOU'RE slapped in the face, spit on, cursed and beat some more.
Could YOU, in this position, have held back YOUR ANGELS that were
ready to KILL ALL HUMANS; standing, at heaven's door ?

Or would YOU have summoned them ?

HUMANS are only filthy creations that YOU had MADE. Would YOU
still have the love in your being, to provided food for them,
and from the sun, cool shade ?

Or in YOUR vindictive heart, would YOU have allowed the ANGELS
you control, to slaughter; every Man, Woman, Son and Daughter ?

Could YOU have endured the pain?
The pain that JESUS took ?

Could YOU have been NAILED upon a cross and hoisted up and
looked; upon the many faces. The ugly, dumb, vain, and pretty
All the faces YOU had made; watching YOU die, without pity.

Would YOU have cursed them ? Made them shriek in immense,
torturous pain ? Would YOU have drained the world and NEVER
made it rain again ? Would YOU have made every MAN on earth,
attack and kill his Son ?

Every Woman and Girl to writhe about in the dirt;
and torture them all just for fun ?

Could upon YOUR death; YOU throw the dead and buried up and out,
into the air. Will the clouds and the skies, cry out for you,
because YOU lost YOUR life down here ?

I don't know, I just don't think so.

So who the hell do WE think WE are ?
With OUR attitudes, trying to be rude.
A tiny vapor is all human life is.

Here one minute and gone the next.
All written in proof in the BIBLE TEXT.

WE THE EVIL.

Running and trying to find this and that,
the things that are so foolishly important to US.

Milling about, working, playing, eating, fucking, or watching TV.
LIFE. - DOESN'T ANYONE GET IT !?
There's so much more to it!

Open your eyes and look past the veil,
ignore EVIL-LUTION, believe in a different tale.

The one about JESUS CHRIST.

No, none of us could have taken the painful
death like JESUS.

So the next time you think your problems are bad,
read this poem and you may feel glad,

or maybe a bit sad,

that JESUS died for you in this horrible way.

Would YOU have done it for HIM ?

GOD'S SHOES

i dreamt one night i stood as tall as a mountain and could see
over all the world

i saw all the tears everyone has ever cried
      there was moisture to form an ocean

i heard all the laughs people have ever laughed
      there was a level That produced an earthquake

i felt all the true love that people have given to each other
      there was luminescence to light the sun.

i smelled all the blood ever shed by hatred
      an acrid, rusty smell that drove all things away into hiding
      and called all scavengers out to feast

i shook the hand of every man
      and kissed every woman on the cheek

i played catch with every little boy
      and skipped rope with every little girl

i walked through everyone's house and witnessed them
      in all acts from vile up to saintly.

i even listened to some of their inner thoughts
      and what they dreamed of daily

i felt their joys and their pains
      from the rich down to the homeless,

            then **i** pondered for a moment..................

               Why ?

(oh gawd, such gratuitous use of the little "i"..)

IF I WERE GOD

If I were God, and had the size, I would sit
on the curve of the moon, to pluck the stars
from the skies, and to you, each one,
I would name.

With my great strength, for you, challenge
a lion and make a warm coat from his mane

With this coat, I would place about your slender
shoulders, to keep you warm as I touch your hand
and we both rise towards space,

Soaring to the heavens, with beauty and grace,
far away for you to notice, that all creations were
spread out in the form of your lovely face.

We would be married in the presence of angels,
who would blow trumpets and sing songs,

We would love each other forever, in a bond,
of eternity long.

And all things would be yours under the heavens
and stars above,

But, since I'm not God and cannot do these things
you'll have to satisfy with just my love.

Kissed as Spirits

Before I knew you in Person
I knew you as a Spirit.

And because spirits have no age,
I remembered waiting for you
behind a golden door; for you
to be created and shared with
the rest of all of existence.

And when you were revealed,
it was so brilliant and bright

There was so much love and light,
that a portion of it was burned into me
for all of eternity.

And we played as spirits
with the many Angels amongst the clouds.
You were so much fun and funny, and sunny,
that those traits followed you down to here
to where you are now.

I remembered looking at you,
way, way, way back then,
And seeing how perfect you were made.

The most beautiful entity that flew.

All the chorus in choir practice, knew,
When you exhaled your grace to lift up
your voice in rejoice.

We all wanted to know your name.

I snuck a kiss in on you once, then
as a spirit. – Because, I just couldn't
help myself in wanting and wondering
what it would be like,
to be as close to you
as I possibly could.
(but this broke the rules…)

We were warned not to do that by God,
but never told why. *(as usual.)*

And it was <u>because</u>, if we kissed as spirits,
we would also kiss in REAL LIFE.

And the chances were, our lives that we
agreed to uphold, may not be perfect.

We were made to be lower than what
we once were. And our unsure, unstable feelings
may get hurt, trampled upon, or get in the way.

When we kissed as spirits,
A white-flash took over both of our minds.
We were welded together for all of time.

I could see everything that you would
eventually do.   Good … bad.

I could feel all the pain
see your struggles
know your disappointments
and taste the salt of your tears.

I knew I was in love with you *(– Then –)*

And then –
You tried on your human skin –

I made up my mind,
I had to exist solely in your era of time.

Even if I were made a dog
and you were a Great White Shark
I would have swum the ocean
to feed you – me – on a hungry day

Because I loved you way back then
and have loved you always ever since.

For over time, I have died with
your name as the last word on my lips,
time after time, until we met
in this current CODA.

_____ *(CODA – cross of dimensional activity…)*

In Heaven,
we were eventually sent down the
long corridor of existence.

And I lost sight of you in the crowd.
I remember calling out your name
and feeling my own tears well up
as my hand reached, grabbed, clutched and shoved
away many others who stood in my way.

My nerves finally burst and I eventually
screamed your precious name for all the
Angels to turn around to look at me with
cold-blank-empty stare, mind washed stares.

The games were done.
And then everything vanished.
Gone.

It was bright again-eye blinding

so bright, I couldn't see anything
around in the surround.

I was being held down – by giants
wearing masks, as they were using
the dullest weapons against me,
that it so tickled rather than hurt.

All they seemed to do was look
at me, make stupid noises and smile.

There I lay screaming your name and
they didn't understand not one word
of what I was saying to them, that I
wanted you. I had been born in skin *(and sin...)*

Though, I didn't know.

I was short, fat, bald, fidgety and
cranky-pissed off as hell.

No one could guess or even tell,
the future or return of my fate.

And all I knew,
was I had a lot of growing to do.

And it would be so long,

forever it so seemed –

before I could try to find you

See your precious face

looking into the eyes that you
had decided to wear down here

and be so close to you again,

as that day

We kissed as Spirits.

Life Keeps Going…

The invent of   this is to celebrate
the living
because when we apply one thought towards
the truest of truths.. the fact is – Life keeps going.

our memory shapes the paths
to the one we lost in the flesh
but never from the heart

our future flows from our past and
with those fond memories of them
thus rends forward the dearly-departed's
reward.

In this scope, no one truly dies

Just as God can and does know
when a sparrow or a crow
falls from the skies
the tears we cry
from the saddened, red eye
makes us realize

we humans were made to suffer loss

we love at a definite cost

and can be connected much deeper
than congested traffic on a freeway

allow me to say

have some ease in your soul
when faced with letting go
know

the soon to be freed
will soon be free

leaving a remainder
here
still happy and dear

that you remain with us
and will be for a while

This plane will give
it will take
it may allow

it will provide new friends

while requiring the tickets
of the old ones

and short of deformity
provides two hands to
negotiate effectively

the

exchange

The most beautiful girl in the entire world

I would love to take you out and treat you like the princess that you hold yourself to be. I want to be in your presence and witness your curiosity, your excitement, your infectious smile.

I want just to hold your hand, if you'll allow me to and to walk with you quietly or as you talk.

I want to come to you, with all the hopes, fears and anticipation of asking you out for any date.

I want to experience the tension of the silent moments and getting through them till speaking.

I would wait, wonder, suffer and continue, this time of wondering if you may ever be mine, until it was all over. And maybe, if it may never come to be at all.

How good the fear feels to know that you are the object of my extreme weakness. How comforting it is to know, that by you, I am totally, completely and unanimously humbled.

How wonderful it is to be forgiven by you and realize the complexity of your gracious heart.

I feel that with the large capacity of time, space and placement - our paths intersected for a reason, and the feelings I have, though they are mine to bear; I will do so to the best of my ability, until you maybe one day deem it not necessary.

Respectfully I say, You are in control. I trust you. And I don't think you would have it any other way.

I just think you are the most beautiful girl in the entire world.

Or maybe, in just my small existence, but It makes me ecstatic to exist just the same. I have felt your sternness and witness your indifference, I have sat quietly as others enjoyed your company and your intoxicating presence and it felt as though I were lit on fire.

And all I can do, is be happy when I am standing in front of you, fumbling for any words to say to hold your interest. Can you understand, a little fear can be a good thing? As when you once said how nervous I made you. Ha? If only you knew how nervous you make me.

In my eyes, you could never do anything wrong. I have never witness one as flawless as you.

*In personality, in dedication, in commitments and in foresight
In posture, in presence, in passion and in power
In character, in integrity, in intellect and in control
In aura, in awe, in accuracy, in inspiration and attention*

You are the most unique person who I have ever met and personally known.

Whoever you are.

93

Old Folks

The old folks had it so much harder.
Yet, as we grew, we thought we were
smarter, and every generation that
comes along, thinks that they are that
much better, than the ones who had
laboriously bore them before.

When there was nothing, to a point
where your partner meant everything,
only then was there true meaning
to being "in a relationship."

The older folks had it worse, and yet,
they felt, what appears to be, the deepest
in "meaningful," love.

It came at a time where, working was
the equivalent to television, there
really was nothing to covet, but your
neighbors land, the world had not
yet been, but eventually went to war,
(twice,) and more people died in an
era of existence than had lived in
the entire spance.

So, here we are, a product of this
and we have everything to a point
of gluttony, yet, we can't seem to
work out the differences to be happy.

It sometimes amazes me – at the level
of human greed and the impoverishment
of the human soul. I know I argue and
rant against the small things that make
life worthy and or possible at times.

So, I can only blame myself, when some
one else is trying so hard to love me, to
not seek a way to make things right.

But, caving in to demands is not the way,
the old folks didn't do that, nor was buying
the world, it never made anyone truly happy
especially when it all fades away anyway.

So, what is the secret to everlasting love?
To a dedication that spans years and decades?
To a point where, two people don't care if
they walk down the street in plaid polyester
and wobble along to get the newspaper and
a cup of coffee, knowing that that may be
the last moment of time they spend together.

Maybe that was the reward to the old folks
who had it so hard and broke, bled and died
to prop up the world that we now take for
granted, leaving a stain, that the young
cannot wipe away in the reach and failure
of hollow loves, based on toys, rather than
futures.

There are quite a few oxymora's in existence,
such as, "girl" "friend," and "old," "fool,"
no one old, gets old by being a fool.

When I see the crumpled couple walking down
the block, I know in my mind, that they know
more than me; at survival, at world events
and at loving someone the other, no matter
what they look like, how much money they
have, what wrong thing they said in 1975
or what seems better at the moment.

No one my age is going to experience that
depth of connection, but it doesn't mean,
no one my age doesn't want to.

It just takes finding someone who's either
not worldly, ultra-forgiving, dedicated,
understanding, wanting, and willing to

spend the time and learn and grow along
the way.

Maybe all the old fools are dead, taken or
gone. And all we are left with, is the Hollywood
translation - of glitter and falsehoods,
or the
Internet inspiration of disconnections and
so many pages to flip of faces in the crowd
that we slip on relationships like black ice
in left or right screen swipes.

The old never had technology, they didn't
need to really, they simply had each other.

And sometimes, I just wish I were old.

The Old Pressed Rose

Its' delicacy and softness, radiates beauty
in the shortness of its life.

Yet the meaning of its' purpose has
remained timeless.

Comparable to circumstance;
a natural day in its' life of
opening,
can reveal so much
in an array of ambrosial
splendor.

The unfolding in offset sequence,
of each and every tear shaped petal,
equivalents the interactions and in-depth
involvements of a relationship.

Beginning largely in involvement
abounding in a closely covered nucleus
of commitment, caring and love.

Adorned with the sweetness of
the progression of love,
we keep these precious symbols as reminders of the
stages of our relationships,
pressed in a book.

It is so we never forget the special moments that lead to
today or to remember, in times of strife, that your loved
one always cares.
No matter their age, their mere existence
and purpose in our lives are the most important.

Comparable to us, my love, like the folds of a rose,
our relationship was delicate, but it withstood through the
tests of time; which curved the ends of the petals, anointed
with scent from the sweetness of our actions.
Like the center of a rose, our relationship
is a tightly bound nucleus of love.

And like the old, our togetherness is now, and forever,
pressed, into the pages of my mind - I love you.

Tiny Boat

If my simple hopes
became a tiny boat

I'd send it afloat
over the ocean of
my tears

to the island that
you sit

where

The sun
that always shines
in the beauty of
your smile

can dry
my puffy eyes
and make me
feel

alive

what I truly miss
the most
is the key
that

i

foolishly
broke

and that
was
called

your trust

With these hands...

With these hands, I have done great and many things.

These hands have solved many problems
Assembled many puzzles
Created many projects
Hoisted great weights
Cradled a small child.

But, never had these hands know any greater pleasure than
your touch to them.

Never had they known anything, like the smoothness of your
precious skin.

Nor the softness of your beautiful hair, where they loved to
hide themselves.

But, now these hands are folded in waiting;
waiting until the day that they
can be encircled around you again.

They are constantly at work,
striving to achieve that
ultimate dream.

My eyes have adored you,
but the hands,
are what actually
sees.

So they say, the eyes are the windows to the soul
but, the hands are the eyes to the whole.

And mine are still waiting
to hold you again.

WOMEN

There's a sparkle
There's a glow

An aura that just shows,
that I want you all to know

About.

Nothing man has made,
Comes close, even just a shade,

To the beauty of a woman, inside, out.

Women, it's to you all, that I dedicate
these words from my pen.

God's detail in you all, is a complex work
of art, that simply fascinates me to no end.

Her eyes are like windows to a warm, exciting
place.

Her walk, an entrancing motion of sex appeal
and grace.

Her teeth are the gate keepers to a music box
from the soul.

Her smile, a ray of sunshine, when directed
melts hearts of stone.

Her laughter is a melody, a missing music
sheet to a symphony song.

Her skin, smooth and precious, and to the
touch, so soft and warm.

Her body, when well-shaped, keeps me
truly, simply dazed.

To interact with these holy creatures,
I'm always just amazed.

There are places on her marked
"Kiss me"

There are areas that whisper
"Caress here"

To choose from you all is such a chore,
far worse than a kid in a candy store.

She is the jigsaw piece to the puzzle that fits.

Yin to Yang.

God, how I love you all.

Post Script:

WOMEN

perfections

Breath taking statuettes of intricacy, colorfulness and beauty.

It is no wonder wars have been fought over you.

Everything in this world is made to catch your eyes.

Angels of heaven themselves weakened to have you. (Gen: 6)

Without you, man-child, would be utter slobs

(However, there are times that I would like my RIB back !)

A fact from the "Male Handbook of Confidentiality".

Women - II

Are the softest things a man can behold.
The essence and denominator of breath-success.

The Yin to Yang – and Yin, of course, is a good thing.

Equally beautiful, as annoying, as confusing, as necessary,
as comforting, as .., as ..., as .. These as's could easily become
the six degrees of separation game for the entire English language.

Women? Truly are mesmerizing – Yet no man, or few men –
especially now, will bear their soul to admit to this.

It's the old, starve 'em, into submission-control game, that I never
got too good at, so my naked heart will just have to do.

I've loved many beautiful women, but even if it was just
three, then I would count myself two times, too lucky.

Imagine winning the lottery three times in your life?
You'd say you were blessed.

Have I ever been mad at you all?
Cursed you?
Hurt any of you? Hell-Yes I have.
Am I sorry?
I apologize for all men, for as I grow in mind, emotions and pants size,
I realize; to say yes – We need to spend more time, figuring things out
about you.

This world and everything in it, is yours –

Women –

There's something so uniquely beautiful about each and every one.
No matter how old, or how used or how abused,
No matter what race or deformity.

Women are God's version of living, loving flowers

– They wake …

Slowly,

Delicately …. stretch,
blinking their eyes like the spreading petals of the morning welcome.

They gently lick their lips, as if tasting the moisturizing dew.
Turn silently, to place feet pads to the floor, in order to add to
what already has been perfected.

Bashful –

You can't see them, till they're ready.

Ever present salesperson –

Always wanting to give the best presentation.

Savior –

When they cook a meal from scratch and it tasted as though it came from
God's kitchen, because it did.

Heart Mender –

When after you've screwed up, lost big, feel ashamed, blew it royal.
They permeate your proximity – a glaze with love in their eyes,
        Scent of their skin –
                Miniature to your frame –

A touch, a hug, a body rub, and say…
        "It's o.k., I still love you, today, as always."
And you know, that's all you need, for another chance to succeed.

Cool as a man tries to be – His guts are knotted inside when she leaves
him,
She doesn't pick up the phone,
Laughs, even platonically with another guy,
Or stares at a Calvin Klein ad too long.

My personal favorite is to brush her hair. Call me whatever …
I don't care.
I've never brushed a guy's hair, and don't plan to.

But what's real magic, is their *interest* –

When they suspend the world in order to understand who you might be.
A six foot, living obelisk standing on Planet Earth. *(Sometimes titled, Planet Wrong)*

Men are a dime a dozen – for without the caress of a woman –
Her voice in the night,
The hope of and reward of fulfilling sex –
Men are living at the lowest level without love.
(Whatever kind in this politically "erect" era.)

Guys, don't get mad at me, these secrets need to be let out the bag –
Cause you'll be the hag, in the end.

A second touting from my pen,
to Women, all corners of the world's-bend,

I wish you all to be my friend?

Yeah right – I want it all.

WOMEN III – The inside…

O.k. let's see, if I were given the world's greatest chemistry set, and told to create a stunningly beautiful woman, what first would I need?
Things that make you go Hmm?

Now mind you the surface stuff comes easy, pretty this and soft that, but what about the person behind the person? Let's start there.

I'd need a light house, to put behind those beautiful brown windows to the soul. The light that shines out and creates life in my dead heart and bows a smile so big on my face, Tonto could shoot a thousand pale faces with it and never break it in.

I would need the exact formula for Tempurpedic foam, to create the elasticity, yet firm supple softness of her well cared for skin, yeah a bunch of minks would do too, but somehow I think she may be a PETA card member and wouldn't go for the skinning
of the little guys.

I would need a skyscraper, o.k. maybe just the frame, because that's how tall she stands against anyone or anything that crosses her.
And how awesome of a sight it is to witness. (I know first-hand)

I would need the mane of a lion, to match her hair to her mood. Washed, cut, softened and styled of course, no animal planet, "direct from the wild" hairdos will do.

I would need a length of steel cable, the type that holds up the Golden Gate should work, need it for her arms and legs, muscles, only lathed down into perfect shapes to match her physique.

I would need the formula for plutonium / uranium to provide just a tiny spark for her megalopolis future.

I would need the world largest library, maybe God's if he's kind enough to lend a key, to provide the supply of her intelligence, intellect, wit, will, conversationalist exposition, and of course plenty of empty shelves for her interests and ability to learn new subjects and retain them for use.

I would steal an Angel's wings right off it's back, *(even in flight,)* then rework them to create her smile.

I would need a sack of gold dust, for that's what she sprinkles into your soul when she acknowledges your existence. (at least mine anyway)

I would need to somehow bottle the essence of a secret between best friends, because that's what it feels like when she crushes you to her body, and throws her weight on top of you in a patented female hug. (A few times I've been so lucky.)
I would need just the reflection of mirror, not the glass, only the properties of, so to mimic the passionate look in her eyes, when she may hear something nice being said about her. Like hopefully this prose.

I would need the tenacity of a wolverine, cause this is how dedicated she can get.

I would need the adhesiveness of welded metal, for if you are a friend to her, this bond is broken just as easily as (which it isn't easy), is just as strong as described and she will react as hot as a new weld or as cold as a cooled weld to something said out of character.
(I don't suggest treading on this one, my personal experience)

I would need the patience of a snail, not in a hurry, calm and on track, never in a rush, at ease with where she is, where she's going, and yet, it drives impetuous nerds like me crazy.

Can't forget the presence of a butterfly in flight, something you will take time away from just about anything to follow with your eyes, maybe playfully chase and try to capture –
– for your own to behold, hopefully forever.

Must include the tenderness and frailty of an embryo, because even though a woman can be all of these magnificent things, she still carries herself with a level of openness and vulnerability and may have been foolishly been hurt in the past by a number of fools.

Now there has to be the ambience of a warm fire on a cold day, because that's how inviting it is to enter her presence and have her accept you.

Bottle up the shockwave from the San Andréaus fault, maybe just a two or three pointer, cause that's how I felt when she first said a word to me with the voice that is:

The missing music sheet that the Angels are ripping apart Heaven looking for, but can't seem to find. Must have been symphony music with a touch of Jew's Harp, but how I love the accent just the same.

Ad an explosion of fireworks, not cheap ones either, Gucci-works over the Brooklyn bridge on fourth of July is for when you catch her off guard, surprise her with a phrase, or make her bust out in laughter. This is how animated her face can sometimes often light up.

Try a dash of the wind, for this is how quietly she walks and how coolly it is when she moves. How softly she steps, and how silent she appears and then is gone. How mysterious it is to see her and then how much she is missed when she is out of sight.

How dry, hot, and slow things are when she is not there and how welcomed and rejoiced things are when she appears again. So vastly important accepted and loved that a full blast of her in the face can make your eyes water.

What about the amperage of 110 volts, not enough to kill you, but enough to let you know she is touching you when she tries to rub ink off your hands with her own.

(Another personal experience.)

How about a measure of depth, again, ported to the touch, for she rubbed my back in a full spring jacket, clothes and all, and her touch felt to me as though I were standing there stark naked.

The mentality of a Mother grizzly, for her dedication to her blood-family.

Insert the giddiness of an otter, swimming around in the ocean, playing with his pals, this is her ability to add to a joke, one up you in a crowd or just have a good time, even when she doesn't feel up to it. Otter? O.k., maybe not that silly.

What about the psychology behind a Military barracks, air force of course, this describes her cleanliness, clean grooming, polish and female maintenance that I can only describe from first-hand experience as being the absolute spotless and germ free clean environment, that carries a penalty of fifty push-ups if it wasn't unilaterally correct.

She's perfect.

Might I add, a touch of burning "Super Nova," cause this is what my heart feels like after feeling like, somehow, I've screwed things up so bad, that she'll never find it in her graces to speak to me again, knowing I screwed up a possible date, upsetting her, and on the same token, knowing everything is o.k. (*The burn first, then snow flurries afterwards.*)

How about a bit of the unknown, like the eerie silence before a storm. My own personal fear of never getting to fully know her and just how wonderful she was made to be. That nerve-chill sickening feeling equivalent to slipping on ice, or walking on a building ledge ten stories up, because I may never hold her hand, share time, a kiss, emotions, laughter, joy or success like I know I would challenge the world with all it took in wanting to.

But finally, the things that I must add into this is, the pull you in personality similar to the suction of a Black Hole, the mysterious, power, birth and endlessness to her levels of understanding - an ocean whirlpool, and (what the heck) the spance, depth and expansion of the mega-verse to tell tale of her enormously vast Heart. Strong, forgiving, desirable, compassionate and beautiful.

What can I say about all of you precious flowers of life,
other than
you are all truly,
ones in a billions.

A Word Picture of Her
(redacted)

First off, this is not poetry, really – if anything is such…
(maybe, when it rhymes too much…)
So, there are few if any rhymes here…
That shit doesn't hafta happen… all the time.

This is as close to a description of love, as close as universal as one can get;
a case study… maybe.
Forget your dog love or love of pizza –
this is about human love and to further clarify, because this is stated and
situated from a right-thinking, procreating male perspective … so it's for a
woman, maybe a particular one or one in an aforementioned circa –
_____

It's as though you are tired, but you actually are not.
a flurry of sugar crazed ants scurry up and down your spine and intertwine
within your rib cage someone must have lodged an exercise ball under your
diaphragm – because it feels like it's inflated upwards against the lungs and
breathing around that special someone is nearly impossible.

speaking on which, where did that tiny-hole pricked through the wall of the left
ventricle of my heart or soul and a steady stream of greasy crystals (crystals and
grease?) seems to release from inside my being and ooze slowly, bubbling inside
– it is such a gut sick, silly feeling that is gnawing and pleasurable all at the same
time

matched only to the Monarch Butterflies in migration inside my chest, where
did the Japanese Hornets come from that sparked their never-ending orgy?

Those fuckers are flying around at drunken speeds and stinging the living shit
out of each other and my inner linings every time I see her

When I finally witness just how gorgeous she is, King Kong must have broken his
chains and rampaged on the loose, grabbed me by the neck and punched me in
the back, general weakness sets in after that, overcoming me like I was fighting
for dear life against a platoon of wild baboons – when I see her, I can't breathe

My tongue must have taken a magic carpet trip, to India or the far, dry desert
East, cause seeing her dries my mouth like a miniature black hole for moisture,
cracked lips and swallowing feel worst that gulping down a whole loaf of week-
old pumpernickel

Is that bad? Not bad enough; some gremlins in two seconds coat your tongue with shellac, that sticks your words to the roof of your mouth like hot tar and renders it harder and coarser to speak than your feet, dry from a long day at the beach

Mind you – you haven't even said anything to catch each other's eye as of yet. This is all just on general recognition and more than likely, it's only one sided.

When you do see them, some precocious five-year-old is silently holding your upper lip in the stupidest "Joker smile" they can put on you, until your face starts to hurt and other's think you are just plain up fuckin weird

I, as well as many, can know they are in love when there exists this constant beginning of tears puddled to the side of my eyes, in just thinking about her, knowing I will see her soon, contemplating the sound of her voice or the softness of her caress – is there anything more of to be blessed?

It's never psychologically sound, especially in talking with yourself out loud, but as I've gotten older, I've had whole loving conversations to complete with laughter and I loves you towards an empty sofa, chair or pillow
- yes, I know, I am the saddest, broken tool-of-a-fool.

I don't care how strong you are – I don't care if you can deadlift the universe
– I don't care if you killed everyone in the last prison you were in

if you truly love someone – as I have and do – this feeling will curl you up, put you down, crush your gut and give you waves of joy when she arrives
– that is the soul turning its key in that perfectly fit hole

funny – when I kiss her – I see stars, a total mess of galaxy splash and colors and crescendo bursts of confusion which smooths out to a high-line Mercedes cruising on a desolate highway with the top down and a tank full of vacation gas, then subsides as if a giant cork were fit over a volcano for next eruption

I know – would have been better if I rhymed it
– what kind of God designs shit like this?

Who can get any work done or an ounce of REM sleep when they feel this way and the love of your life is right next to you. Who can deny that love is the absolutely strongest, strangest gravity ever discovered or experienced, but never explained.

My heart is spilling out, because I did truly love someone who I have tried and tried and tried to describe
-    but as she does, so does her definition, elude me.

I rarely do this – I will truncate the rest and spare you this mess, because this one was a very long anthem to a time that still confuses me and just may as well only serve to confuse you too.

Love –

will make a man work three jobs for his family
will make a woman cook clean or turn to the streets
will make a soldier cover a grenade for his comrades
will make a man in China, stand down a tank (he had to love something...)

Let us not forget, that life is not only, food and drink, work and grind
I like to say – we are not here on a punish assignment, though it seems
like it and we just end up sometimes punishing each other.

Look at someone else and find the most excellent best good in them.

Look at someone else – and try to even feel just a few lines – as I once have
it's the greatest feeling – especially for someone who feels not one thing.

Post Script:

Obtaining the world to give to someone is truly a steep challenge. Finding someone worthwhile to actually hand it to, is something uniquely and completely different ... and so much more of a challenge.

Whoever Holds This Book…

The shine of it
The pride in it
has a piece of my heart;
for what it's worth

It is my heart
a great example
yeah, yeah, yeah
tattered
shattered
remainder of a retelling
in the reminder to
my state of being.

the tide we're all caught up in
and where we might be going

situations that challenged it
changed it, forbade it and
torched it black completely

all these fun little chemical
emotions and proportions to
measured portions of potions
that it seemingly took to pull
me up out of
"Can't-Wipe-my-own-ass,"
street

to the slivery plateau on which
I teeter, if sometimes stand

This book is the story of how
one beautiful, simple, humble
predictable and maybe in some
way loveable woman, created
a man far outside the womb

another greatest story never told
until now

bear witness to these brush
strokes, see the typed keys
being depressed

to which leave some stuck
and recessed

the pages are my life, heart
and soul behind my very green
eyes

and each chapter after; a pathway
took without her

as I've mentioned a hundred
million times, all good things
come to an end   (stings)

I'm a no face in the crowd
an-every type "Grey man,"
a brown spot on the
sand like an entrenched
hungry grouper

But, inside I rule a world
from her guidance and
influence

an input that seemed to
so far stand the test and
a passing maze of days

to the unworthy who hold
this book, look, steal it like
gold and burn it inside your
soul – maybe you'll realize
you're far from being alone
feeling awkward and seeing
the canopy of life universally

love (at least hopefully mine,)
never gets old – it only deepens
it's roots and has become the
tiny little Achilles Heals of my
white-whine-spilled tears

This book is me – facing my bleached
future, with all the uncertainty
like any other before me – of that
darkened curtain pull and bow out
that awaits us all

but with the strings tightly
drawn and no view behind
door number one –
I continue to try to have fun and expose
whatever good to any who will
read   seek   maybe listen
make changes
turn their direction
for new expression

too many words huh?

Become part, if not all of the
solution and look away from
the problem

this story hopefully shows
that the dog can eventually
find his day, if he will watch
and wait, dodge cars and be
openly aware and completely
fair

in his or her decisions

Nova Bougie

Stereotypes

A cheesy black guy, one day asked me,
"Me'an, why I ain't got no job?"
See, at the time, I had two, and
I was doing quite well.

Hmm, I thought, have you ever tried
to speak like a normal person?

Or clean up your image?

Oh, you want to be an individual,
I understand, now I see.
Then don't expect what's normal.

I'm fully aware of the Fifth Amendment.
To plead the fifth, allows against self
persecution, and no one likes to implicate
themselves, especially those who fear
the truth.
No more George Washingtons
or honest Abes anymore.

So, let me spin the truth –

Why don't cops like Black guys?
Why don't we have a Respect the Homeless day?
Why do hoes sometimes not get paid?
Seriously, why don't super models date
obese iron workers?

And the list goes on, but you get my point,
it's a little long word called Stereotypes.

So, my advice, - look around you.
I'm no great fan of society, but, trying
to live outside of it, is like a fish, living
in an apartment on Fifth Avenue.

Now, it's not impossible, but there's
what's practical and probable.

Clean up your act.
Straighten your attitude,
fuck the individualism, and the
heritage, cause like a wise old
black man once told me –
   "Black Power'll get you killed."

Speak right.
Enunciate.

Dress well, don't be a target.

Find some goals, don't slouch
to the lowest denominator of
life, or you may find that you'll
never get back up.

Care – about yourself,
because the day you
say you don't very few
will say they will.

Don't play around with matters of the
heart. Yes, hurt people - hurt people,
but you may unlock a vault of retribution
against yourself that no one can see,
and only Karma can throw those blows
and what I've found out in life is,
she's got deadly dam good aim.

Your job for success, is to know your
stereotype. To know what people
associate you with. Sure, you can say
you don't give a shit, and you don't
care, but a greater plan of control
was hatch against you so long ago.

And now, you can only revolve around
it, like the moon around the Earth.
Don't get it twisted, don't be a fool.

Even the good book says, *knowledge is power,*
and when the thief realizes his actions, let
the thief steal no more, but come into the
goodness of his knowledge.

My friends, my loves, my family, my strangers,
Know this --
know thyself,
know thy path,
know who stands against you
and definitely know why.

Then know how to get around
it.

Don't be fooled.

Being and individual is great,
if it catches on as a circus act,
but other than that,
it usually leads to nowhere.

Is success in life a bunch of money?
Not necessarily.

It can be a combination of all things
that make life a dream.

Spend time to really know what that
is, and not have that projected on
you by what someone else thinks.

It will be either your thoughts,

or there's.

(and please… it's called a belt to the bootie-crack-showin-ass-saggerz..)

118

WHY CAN'T WE STOP ?

WHY CAN'T WE STOP ?

BLACKS already have it bad enough with the COPS.

Do we need each other on our backs too ?
Why do some of us act like such fools ?

A BLACK MAN can't be RICH,
without being a SELL-OUT.
If he's got something nice,
another brother wants to blow
his brains out.

I'm cruising in my car.
Music playing where I like it at.
I'm eyed by some "nigga" on the curb
like I'm some sorta faggot.

"What are you looking at ?"
goes through my fuckin-mind.
Why can't I just drive,
my car
and have a good time ?

Don't be jealous of me; because I work
my fingers to the
bone.

Don't be mad at me because
I'm blessed, with a beautiful wife,
and a happy home.

Don't step to me thinking, I'm soft
and won't protect myself.

I'm light in the skin. Don't talk much wind.
But ain't afraid to deal pain
to someone who needs it dealt.

WHY CAN'T WE STOP ?

A girl said to me, I wasn't BLACK,
because I spoke much too proper.

"You want to be white!
You ain't down."
I just wanted to slap her.

Being down with what?
People think being BLACK
is just A FAD.
Talking the YANG
Being in a GANG
Or how many babies
"They done HAD."

To me if being WHITE, means having
SENSE, PEACE, and
HAPPINESS in LIFE.

Find a paint brush, and some paint,
and paint me WHITER
than white.

BROTHERS AND SISTERS, read this with a grain of salt.
Where we are TODAY, in the world, is not all, OUR fault.

BUT, you have a brain, you have two feet, two hands, two ears
two eyes, and breathe air. As long as you are life,
there is a chance for you out here

take it
live it
be it

Nothing is impossible, no not shit, don't fear to live in this world,
don't lock yourself in a pit.

And to those who really think being BLACK is: just GUNS, DOPE,
and RUNNING FROM THE COPS; I have one thing to say to YOU,

WHY CAN'T YOU JUST **STOP** !

We are no longer oppressed ...

Just obsessed.
With ghosts of the past.

We are no longer oppressed,
just unwanted guests,
to a feast that no one knows how long will last.

We are no longer held down,
yet we still frown,
while all around, we cause our own calamity.

There are no more riots to join, or walls to breach,
so preachers hold the speech - of the message of unity.

There are no more color lines, in the world of skylines,
where hard times are solely defined by your education level,
to your Bank account level – and well, the only color now is
Green.

A Black man won't run this country any better than a White man,
nor would a Woman, because they are all Human and fallible to
personal interests and bias.

So we are no longer oppressed,
Because the only civil unrest, now exists inside our own homes.

Where the man is no longer King and his input means nothing,
he can be removed with a phone call, and this destroys all,
while the woman now does her thing which includes children
but no male discipline.

And the Bible clearly says, "Spare the child, not the rod."

So, the nucleus family sits destroyed, by gay marriage and
Laws, yet we want to say that we as a race still need a path
created for us.

It is time to stop being Black People and just call ourselves,

People.   *(The year 2020 made me change my thinking, entirely...)*

Dial "I" for Impulse

Let's get real and fuckin face it,
this world we live in is not aseptic
nor as clean a sunny bunny-fuck-pad
green screen that every Queer and
every Queen friendly, we're-your-buddy
newscaster lightheartedly seems to predict

I'm gonna spell it out quick, least we
forget, that "this world" was forged
and is steeped in the iron-hemoglobin
of the previously conquered, enslaved,
nationally brave and heroic-stoics

ahh, their memories live on in stone
monuments, metal wall plaques and
mausoleum plots – I hear the laughter
of my neighbor as I type this--, just
wanted to include to add dimension
that the world is constantly spinning,
-- while I'm crying, she's out there
grinning, laughing and chattering on
in Tagalog

why is this one not in the Bad
how did it miss the Grey, because
those areas would be too Bougie,
and this one is the neva of nevas

This time of sitting at home allows
me to envision and relive so many
occurrences that it's not funny
and I must resound to the fact
that my resolve is set to a bar
so high that I feel my life is on
auto-pilot - non-default to fail

it doesn't mean I haven't peeked
once or twice over the rails – of
indifference and "feeling" as though
I had run out of luck or lost my way.

Do people not believe or see that
sometimes they can go too far and use
the wrong person or chaff against
someone or something way more
abrasive than they ever dreamed

122

Society forgets, that many are only a
living, gravity-suspended bag of water
and wasted time – cogs in the machine
turning at different speeds and greasing
each other en motion

In my years and now I can finally say,
they have been many; I have learned
lessons I never knew would or could
exists, changed my mind a few times
of things I believed where the iron
gates of neither passage and enjoyed
pleasures, both prohibited, stolen
and subdued by knowledge of only
shadowed learning.

So what am I really saying - you bet
your ass I had many times when the
thought crossed my mind to kill someone.
Is it plain enough in type for you to see?

You hear about these hillbilly
po-dunk places, where Larry-Joe
offed Joe Shmoe for a taste of
his wife – Geez, that happens
quite often in the big city too.

Women tell men, "Why don't you
just be a man and accept any
amount of bullshit I can throw,
give, do or put upon you –

I once responded that men are
not donkeys to be saddled with
foolery and misuse –

the lesson to be studied is the sheer
fact, that in the days of old and even
recent, when men wanted something,
they grouped together, rowed out in
boats and killed everyone on the other
side to get what they wanted –

enslaving and assimilating or plain
full wiped out the conquered.

These notions where reserved for
Kings and Popes, but still, the same
fire that burnt in their balls also
crackles in mine.

This is a likened tale, exposed in code
because my hurts are so recent and
hurts give birth to those murderous
tendencies.

How about when you're working and
making a living and someone called
"a boss" – (only by attrition and level
of dust on their necks...)
makes life and daily living – excruciating

Where do you think the term – "going
Postal," came from – a cleansing of certain
folks that had sat around on their keisters;
played god too often, too long and too
many times with the wrong person who
said fuck you if you take away my lively
hood –

look, I'm certainly not saying that
everyone is in the right and murder
should be done every Wednesday
night like it was a weekly purge

I am addressing that there are legitimate
and necessary urges that fulfill needs, like
sex, eating, buying a car, toilet use, etc.

A solid, 4D printed fact is that more guns
exist in the great U.S.A than people, but that
simple pleasure is way too quick referenced
as by a classic villain, the knife affords a look
into the many nuanced grimaces of pain

poisons have been the old-age equalizer from
Biblical and BC days even carrying on to
modern times with spores grown in labs
then released in bat markets

don't look down on me for verbalizing the truth
there will always be a reason, feel or need to
dial "I" for impulse

LIES
(are daggers and knives…)

Nothing really hurts worse, than when you've been used.
Nothing feel worse that when you're lied to and can't obtain
the truth. Lied to by someone you loved and trusted and had
tons of faith in, that's hard for you to conjure up for anyone.

This one is a fresh wound, because the blood spurting from
my heart is arterial-Rembrandt-cherry and I'm crying daily.

Lies, from the right person, can cut deep and wound like daggers
and knives; I thought I was good with words and using them
as weapons, but nothing takes the cake as having your insides
splayed with your own hopes and anticipations crumbling
down inside of your stomach like glass impregnated lead.

How does one describe that? Even with all my "likes" and
"as" and "such," I just still can't sum it up. Here is a distinct
portion of this story, I remember clearly, the last time I knew
that my father loved me – and that was when *I told him a lie*.

I was all of five.

I don't remember what it was about, but I do remember saying,
"And you believe me?" trust me (if you can,) my father was not
by any means a good man, but I guess all scum have a silver lining
when he simply replied back to me.

"If you say so, then why would I not believe you." This was trust.

So, if I inadvertently at that time knew the feeling in the easiness
of deceptively getting away with something small, how are kids
ever regarded as innocent little beings at all?

How things can and often will come back to us. Please share this
moment with me, my self-therapy, as I am in utter nuclear waste
level containment of so much internal pain. Had I fully known the
boomerang effect, I would have my lived my previous life as a saint.

I'm suffering this ripped open chest feeling with castor oil consistency
seeping from my heart, I have to really wonder, just how many more
of these moments will I have to eventually go through.

24-hours

I'm not smart
certainly not patient
and saddled with this truth for a long time

some wonder, about what others do, pull off
achieve, accomplish – don't you hate when I
use more than one word – just trying to take
up space or make a point

if those words were seconds in a day, then
they would not go to waste, because they
were being put to some sort of use

my statement, direct; there is one thing that
one marvels at in another, and wonders why
they can't "obtain" the same or scratched their
heads in pondering the thoughts in the tenacity
of someone's success

the rich, the poor, the lost (at least above
ground) all have the same time of length;
24-hours to throw around

might sound silly, obliviously-obvious, but
that's the lowest, low common denominator
of the human condition

what a person does with their time is what
they produce into the fine wine of their
labor or the bitter whine of their sorrows

this one might sound a little punchy and
clunky, but it's 5 in the morning, so you
can take a random guess at what I spend
my time doing

from the U.S. President, to a pauper in the
street to a Joe-average working slave, we all
share this empty and intangible, immovable
yet totally consumable "bottle" that we are
seemingly locked into

some complain there is not enough time,
yes, there is; others say, time goes too fast
slow down and watch it with your eyes

many say they waste time or do not
waste time, then try expanding horizons
by investing in something "time-producing"
so a reward of time comes back to you

I (and yes... I finally get to my 1st person view,)
can't see how people just aren't hopping mad
about how life and the time designated for it
has been funneled toward the needs, goals and
"money = time"-producing-surplus for the one
percenters

life used to be "time" was used to support
life, the farm, animal husbandry, working
the fields, seed "time" and harvest "time"

now, it's time for traffic, time to clock in,
time to get to work, break time, lunch-time
time to do shit that shuts off your brain
time to go home, time to be in traffic

dinner time, TV time, repeat

in that cycle, sixty years drains by real
easy; time is a commodity no one can
buy or it would have been all bought up

so please, not for me, matter of fact,
don't listen to me, if you don't want
to I'm fine

My time lane is pretty clear, Tswhy I'm
sitting here, typing and doing what I
want; it was a struggle and lot of time
spent not knowing how things would
turn out, but I had some sort of faith
and that is a different tale all the same

just don't' complain, if you don't have
what you want or covet a celebrity
they don't look at life and time the
way the average do

this was explained in "FISH – II" *(B.S.'s Soul)*
"life mimics the ocean where certain types of fish "live" at the top,
"exists" in the middle or "lurk" at the bottom;"
use time wisely or just give it to me

Tripping through the effects

A number of metaphysical effects shroud existence like the shadowy dark corners of a lit prism. A few are:

The **Andromeda** Effect - A feeling that one has travelled to other universes

The **Astral** Effect – A feeling that one can project themselves outside of their physical bodies

The **Butterfly** Effect – A belief that a butterfly flapping its wings in one spectrum, creates gale force winds on the other side

The **Mandela** Effect – A notion that hearing or seeing a similarity, replaces actual reality

The **Manchurian (*a.k.a,* Monarch)** Effect – mind control with on off switch capability

Déjà vu – feeling as through a time, place or occurrence has been experienced before

Clairvoyance – An ability to see futuristic occurrences or obtain "spiritual knowledge,"

Empath – soul connections based on feelings, sensitivities and some chakra vibrations

Paranormal – physical actions or manifestations produced by demons, ghosts, spirits

hm... how about the **Life** Effects

Where, maybe, our smallest actions will be our greatest movements. The unseen paths that are carved internally, lead to open roads of success, loves, joys and triumphs.

An effect of starting in a nowhere-nothing state of being to attain some understanding of how a personal world works, a committed world works, and a mutually built world works.

The effect of beginning courageous, strong, beautiful, fearless and having that all, slowly metamorphoses into the opposite of all the above mentioned, under a humbling peace, at a crawling pace and imparting impacting lesson-filled acceptances in the process.

Life effect, converts the bearer, slowly in a blanket of academic, sensory, emotional, physical and at some if not most times, consequential theories that seem overbearing with little yield of overcoming and at times offer nothing more than unseen will and silent, unpredictable-inner determination to attempt to make any changes.

The Life Effect is the hardest to muddle or muscle though; a factor of: pursue, reach, stretch, fail, reassemble, begin (a new,) succeed, set back, reset, reattempt, move up, forward, suffer a loss, win, draw, have the bottom fall out, hang on by your finger nails, feel depressed, regroup, find love, lose, cry, die (inside,) stand, smile, repeat, continue...

One day I was really hoping and praying for something good to happen

A job, some money, maybe a girl to notice me...

it was dark and I was lonely with just my hurts accompanying my one and only single-bubble of a dream

when I saw a tiny glint of metal on the opaqueness of the black asphalt;

it was a small, forged, Buddha charm, half-gristled from being run over about a half a dozen times, but there he was, his constant dead pan face and chubby cheeks and Mona Lisa mookie –

suspicions flooded in

what does this mean, if anything

had my Christian coverage lapsed and now I was being farmed out to an emergency tiered-rate company

did Jesus decide to take a shower amid all that sitting at the right-hand that he's supposedly doing

did I mistakenly eat like a pig during Ramadan

it was and still remains, the oddest find in my life - and - at the most peculiar moment in time

needless to say

Buddha failed me too

Quatrain

Like all things have a beginning
so must there be a distinct end.
- *an overlooked observation.*

End means options
new beginnings
and a new beginning leaves sans
room for the old or unwanted.

oh' dwellers; Life makes the
decisions, never you or I.

The greater power that resides
decides whether we live or die

when we came and to whom;
as what in what color or mode.

So let it be told, that life will come
to an end, as of it we currently know.

Now-How

It may revolve around the mass dependency
on other nations and rogue countries.

As one nation, was incredibly intelligent,
to foresee, that of a particular agent,
there was limited quantity.

Now, surely, as you live in your home
and take inventory,
Who better than you to know the balanced
stock of soup to nuts?

So, we gladly sat back,
cars lined up at station for gas
and in a wink of an eye - the glint of a pearly grin,
the secret was finally revealed that the
good ole' U.S.A, had more oil than
piles of sand.

via petrodollar we exchanged so much filthy
green paper for practical, tangible, usable,
burnable, configurable molecules of
black soup ...

We had drunk our fill
and our fill was all the desert.

in that, the sand people tried
desperately to buy back
some of the oil,
only to find that the money they had,
was only good to light an oven
for In God they don't really trust.

With their lights turning off and their
stores going empty, they resort to
trickery as a British force invades to
reclaim the lost territory.

In a valiant-gallant last stand effort
they over reach their hand,
to a small yet pestiferous
neighbor who happens to be beloved
by many, including the one they don't
trust

and thus …

predicts the end of days, black as
the soup it started over.

With the many armies mounting,
towards the tiny stamp of earth
and the stakes growing higher
and ever higher

God himself steps from the sky
and practically walks down the ladder
to reclaim his dearly historic prize
and silence the streams and waters

forever maybe from human eyes.

a stillness is adopted
a peace is assumed
a rebirth is inevitable
and everything is made new.

And this time, there will be no
simp-saips there to fuck it all up.

Anthem to the End

No dedication or realization prompts revelation to
where anyone is going - was - were or where they
may have always been headed

some are like me – I hate the words
us or we; rare does a plural category exist in
abused, lonely, striving or misunderstood
trying to function in the game of "society"
under the designs by the few before that
carved footpaths where they wanted the
rest of the masses to gingerly step

and one (such as) me, who had an inkling
of what was being seen as pretentious
false and fabricated

notions behind sex, gender, success and
politico bullshit to world, sports and pathos-tic
entertainment ... sway was just never part of the
picture

price of a clear head, costs everything - pressing
forward in a world that was pre-designed to
leave the masses struggling behind in confusion
of what to do and who would do it for them –
almost all now penned animals in a cheery little
"we love each other zoo" as the 1 percent chew
grind and rescind them like bush meat to nothing

were the unwanted too smart or just simple-omnivores
with keener vision; had descendant spirits of wolves
and sharks embittered hearts and shape-sharpened
hardened minds of some of the blind forcing these chosen to see

ends are only a different beginning and a new start with
a select few used to bringing about new methods of
being

end means a cleanse of the comfortable and the
settled and the content, the apathetic and contrite
the lazy and the plenty – end means scrub the dirt
which may hurt – like a surgery that cuts away decay

this thought is antecedent in nature to the "everything
is alright, we love each other" folly that has become the
22nd century polly-anistic scenery and possibly soon;
it will be a memory of a seeming utopic time where
money became a computer program and the world
was so tightly-financially locked, that conquest was
done through banks, computers and soy beans

the masses forget – that the ground is only fifty percent
dirt as much is the cobble of splintered bones of the dusty
haggard that trudged the earth before us

soil is seeped in iron of the blood of the slain, the brave
the cowardly – no matter what category – they are all
dead and not even a close or distal memory

no negotiations occurred when one group met a weaker
other than to say – give us your women and your
possessions or face annihilation

so this carbon based creature found a season of diplomacy
and shared an era when everyone could have a small piece
of a pie that they did not bake – so says a good book, that
free tastes well for a while, but the glutton shall perish with
a mouth full of gravel

a wise person I met once uttered – if things are good, you can
know – they will go bad, when things are bad, you can only
hope they go good – so bad is reliable and good is a luxury

end are those days – those days of false loves and universal
universalism – where people tried like rolling a rock uphill
to instill that "Black lives mattered" when only black soup
matters and black death loves everyone

where the masses once were only concerned with how they
looked or appeared on a stupid app screen for a few seconds
before they were swiped right or swiped left and forgotten
like time never knew them – and how true that will be

I write not to others like me – because – I truly don't care if
you exist. I would never want to know or run into one like
me – who swallow no bullshit about the communal and only
seeks the highest ground on ground short stumpy legs.

shunned, lied to, revealing any inner most feelings sparsely
like the sun peeking out from behind hail clouds

having been dispatched and displaced from everywhere at
every turn by everyone and – inside, waiting for these end of
days to come
-- this, will be the end.

an end that shakes loose the pins that held all the cogs in
the wheels

an end that evaporates the falsetto approach to courtesies
or genderisms or plagiarisms – possibly shattering all isms,
ings, ates, ats, and cats

this Anthem of the End marks a nearing of the final time of
a realist's view of the kaleidoscope window of illustration to
things that are believed, except one who held inner thoughts
and refused to wallow in a regurgitate of lies

at some point – life – became a record player that turned
and turned and finally – the record needed to be changed

as any – rational – being – one would hope the decent into madness
would be slow and controlled; avoided completely at all costs

but, I nor anyone like me, made the previous designs of world, life
and strife and – yes, had I been at the top, I would have designed it
to look, act and function just as it had all before and along,
because I would have rode prone atop that glorious wave

had I more to say that might make sense – it would be on this
page – living a life of questioning, struggling, working, waking on
days when they were not worth seeing, buying, selling, fucking
and near dying from having whatever heart or feelings shattered
into pieces from uncaring individuals

for I – it has made me hyper aware, hyper attuned and hyper critical
of the system that can and will change and FORCE you to accept it

The Anthem to the End – says – in the end – will you – accept what
you are given? And this is the only time I will address you, because
I can answer for me – I have not – I will not and I embrace the end
from one who had reached for life many times, only to have his
fingers broken and heart scored a million times for ever wanting
to feel human.

This Anthem to the End is my signature telling myself
– that the end –

can but only last a few moments –

a brave soul once wrote –

"I have come here and have seen enough,"
" I go to now to see the other side –"
" I am not crazy, nor deranged,"
" I am just bored with this all."

To me that was bravery –

that was a stoic Anthem to the End.

PRO

RNG: 150yds   MVL: 2200fps
WND: -21SE   CAL: 30-06
TRJ: ARC   DAM: KIL

An Unabridged Book of Good and Evil

Fear Not...

That no one may ever know your name...

this modern-day-age existence of life

breeds via trials at the trough

toil over money

and scant in the fumes

waifed by

fame

Made in the USA
San Bernardino, CA
17 July 2020

74999901R00084